Florence Marryat

The Hampstead Mystery

Vol. III

Florence Marryat

The Hampstead Mystery
Vol. III

ISBN/EAN: 9783337051969

Printed in Europe, USA, Canada, Australia, Japan

Cover: Foto ©Andreas Hilbeck / pixelio.de

More available books at **www.hansebooks.com**

The Hampstead Mystery.

A Novel.

BY

FLORENCE MARRYAT,

AUTHOR OF 'LOVE'S CONFLICT,' 'VÉRONIQUE,' 'MY OWN
CHILD,' 'MY SISTER THE ACTRESS,' 'HOW LIKE
A WOMAN,' 'PARSON JONES,' ETC., ETC.

IN THREE VOLUMES.
VOL. III.

LONDON:

F. V. WHITE & CO.,
14 BEDFORD STREET, STRAND, W.C.

1894.

THE HAMPSTEAD MYSTERY.

The Hampstead Mystery.

CHAPTER I.

HANNAH HINDES did not know what answer to make to this direct appeal. She was an honest woman, to whom a lie was an abhorrence, but she was also a woman who held her husband's reputation, perhaps his life, in her hands. She hesitated so visibly, that Captain Hindes began to think his brother's disorder must be such as she found it impossible to speak to him upon.

'Well, never mind,' he said presently, 'I see you are unwilling to mention it, but I shall soon get it out of old Hal. But you make me feel rather anxious, Hannah. If my brother has not consulted a doctor, I must make him do so. His health is too

VOL. III.   A

valuable to you and the children to be trifled with. By the way, talking of children, what induced you to send those two little fairies, Elsie and Laurie, away from home to be educated? I thought that was altogether against your principles, Hannah. Edith says she remembers your giving her a long lecture on the subject when Fanny was born, and cautioning her never to let a daughter be educated anywhere but at home. She has dinned it into my ears whenever I have hinted the young lady was old enough to go to school.'

'Yes!" replied Hannah, with a sigh. 'Those have always been my sentiments, Arthur, and are so still. But Henry has grown so irritable of late, that the noise of the children playing about The Hall disturbed him, so I thought it best to let them go. They are with an old friend of mine, where I can see them almost every day. I daresay,' she continued, timidly, 'that you thought it very strange that we could not receive you at The Old Hall, as we did before.

It cost me more than I can tell you to write and put off your coming here. But it was for the same reason. My husband cannot bear the least noise or confusion. I am afraid he has overtaxed his brain, and, when he returns home, he requires absolute rest.'

'Don't say anything more about it,. Hannah,' replied her sister-in-law. 'Of course, Artie and I knew there was some unavoidable reason for the refusal. And, much as we should have liked to renew our former pleasant relations with you, everything must give way to Henry's health.'

'What are your plans?' inquired Hannah.

'We have hardly fixed them yet,' said Captain Hindes. 'We thought of staying in town for a while, just to see a few theatres and other amusements, while we look out for a country cottage to spend the summer in. But if my brother is seriously ill, I shall not dream of going far away from him.'

'Oh, Arthur! he is not so ill as that!' exclaimed Hannah; 'it is his mind that is suffering, rather than his body. He works so hard at the business, and now, of course, everything falls on his shoulders. He seldom gets to the City before noon, and, when be comes home, he is so exhausted, he cares for nothing but to go to bed.'

'But neuralgia is generally due to physical weakness, Hannah. The doctors always give Edie a tonic for it the first thing. Is Hal taking nothing to strengthen him?'

'I don't think he takes anything but morphia when the pain becomes intolerable,' replied Hannah; 'but, Arthur, don't argue with him on the subject. Nothing makes Henry so irritable as to be talked to about his health. When you see him, treat him as if you saw no difference in his appearance. He won't let even *me* mention the subject to him.'

'He must be mightily changed,' said Captain Hindes, sighing; 'however, I will take your advice, and keep silence on the matter. I shall call at his office the first thing to-morrow. When do you think I shall find him there?'

'Not before twelve, Arthur; if then. Will not you and Edith have some refreshment before you go back?'

'No, thank you, Hannah. We are both tired, and should not have moved out except to see you. Tell old Hal all about us when he wakes up, and say I shall be in Sise Lane early to-morrow. Good-night, my dear. I'm awfully sorry about his illness. It's quite spoilt my coming home, but I hope I may be able to cheer him up. If it is due, as you seem to imagine, to his over-working himself, I think I shall be able to persuade him to come out a little with me, and brush the cobwebs off his brain. What need has he to ruin his health by work? He has made plenty of money, to say nothing of the handsome legacy that Mr Crampton left the son and heir. By the way, how is the prodigy? I conclude he has not left home as well as the girls.'

'No,' said Hannah, with a wintry smile;

he is not quite old enough for that yet. He will not be three till his next birthday. He is quite well, thank you, Arthur; but I have to keep him at the top of the house, for fear he should disturb his father.'

'Why, Henry was always so devoted to Master Wally. Edie and I have often laughed together over his letters about his little son, and said, surely no man had ever had a boy before. At one time he could write of nothing else.'

'Oh! yes, and he loves the child as much as ever, perhaps more, but he cannot stand his noise. It jars upon his nerves. Sometimes I long for the time when Wally shall be able to go too. It is a dull life for a young child to be confined to the company of his nurse.'

'You grieve me more and more with each word you say, Hannah,' replied her brother-in-law; 'however, I shall see Henry for myself to-morrow. Come! Edie, we must make tracks for our hotel.'

'Won't you wait for the carriage to

take you back,' asked Hannah anxiously, for she was distressed at not being able to show them more hospitality.

'No, thanks, dear. We shall get home quicker by the Metropolitan. We shall see you again soon. Good-night!' and, with his wife's arm snugly tucked under his own, Captain Hindes walked off again.

As soon as she was sure that they were gone, Hannah sat down and indulged in the luxury of 'a good cry.' It was seldom that she permitted her feelings to get the better of her, but this interview had upset her.

The semi-deceit she had been compelled to practise—the determination of Captain Hindes to find out what was the matter with his brother, and the evident suspicion with which he had received her statements, all combined to make her fear that a crisis of some sort was at hand. She dreaded what her husband might do or say if his brother pressed him too hard for an explanation of the alteration in his demeanour and appearance. His brain was at times so muddled, even in the day-time, that he spoke more like a madman than a sane person, and if Arthur took it upon himself to consult medical men on Henry's behalf, or to have him privately watched, what terrible *dénouement* might not be the consequence. She wished heartily that her brother and sister-in-law had not returned home just at that particular moment, that they had given her time to coax her husband to leave England for awhile, as he had seemed so well disposed to do, but wishing was futile. They were there, in their midst, and she must set all her wits to work to conceal the real state of affairs from them.

She visited her husband's bed-chamber at once, to find him sunk into a slumber, from which she could only rouse him to a semi-torpid condition. So she wisely let him sleep until the morning, when he was able to listen to her story, and conceive a hazy idea that his brother and his wife had paid The Old Hall a visit whilst he was asleep.

When Captain Arthur Hindes walked into the office the following day, he found his brother had not yet arrived. Naturally he was well-known there, by Mr Bloxam and all the older employés of the firm, and he received a hearty welcome, for he was a general favourite. Arthur was taller and fairer than Henry—had a handsomer face and a neater figure—was possessed, moreover, of a bright, happy temperament, and had always a kind word or a jest on hand.

'Not arrived yet?' he exclaimed in answer to Bloxam's intimation of the 'governor's' absence, 'and nearly half-past twelve! What makes him so late, Bloxam? He used to be called· "the early bird" at one time.'

'Ah! Master Arthur, things are changed since then,' replied the old cashier, 'Mr Henry's not been nearly so active of late. I often think he's not well. He seems so mopey and dull. Perhaps it will be different now you've come home, Mr Arthur. You'll cheer him up a bit. He has felt

Mr Crampton's death terribly, and Miss Jenny's too, for the matter of that, they came so quickly, one after the other, and he ought to have taken a change long ago. I'm very glad you've come back, sir. You'll do him more good than anyone else could do.

'I am glad also, Bloxam, for Mrs Hindes's account of him quite alarmed me. But do you think he is really ill?'

'I think he is very, *very* ill, Mr Arthur,' returned Bloxam, mysteriously; 'but here he is, so I will leave you together.'

Saying thus, the cashier retreated by a side door into his particular sanctum, as the glass doors from the front swung slowly on their hinges, as though propelled by an enfeebled hand, to admit Henry Hindes. He entered, looking much as he had always done of late, slouching along with a bent figure and a shaking frame. He had made some attempt, at the instigation of his wife, to brighten up his general appearance by assuming a frock coat and a tall hat, but they only served to make the difference in him more apparent. Captain Hindes could not for a moment believe the evidence of his senses, but when he was convinced that it was his brother who stood before him, he started forward to greet him with a slight cry.

'Good God! Hal, my dear old fellow!' he exclaimed, 'is this you?'

'Who else?' demanded Henry, with an attempt at jocularity, as he held out his hand and grasped that of Arthur.

The younger man looked him in the face for a few minutes without speaking. He could not trust himself to do so. He was too infinitely shocked. *This* Henry? Henry, whose devotion to his personal appearance had passed into a family proverb—who had always been the 'nattiest' youth, and the most perfectly-dressed young man, and the most faultless gentleman in the City—whose irreproachable garb and spotless linen and glossy hats had been cast in his teeth in bygone days, as witnesses that he was not fit for business or anything but a *cavalier des dames*. This limp, untidy, slovenly-looking man, with bloodshot eyes, and unhealthy complexion, his brother Henry, of whom he used to be so proud? Arthur felt a great lump rise in his throat, and could have sat down and cried to see the difference a few years had made in him. But he held his hand as in a vice instead, and replied in as hearty a voice as he could manage,—

'Why, dear old chap, you're not looking yourself at all. You took me quite by surprise, though Hannah did prepare Edie and me last night to see a change in you.'

'Hannah, Hannah!' cried his brother quickly; 'what had she to say of me? What did she tell you? How dared she— I mean, why did she mention me at all?'

'My dear Henry, it would have been very extraordinary, surely, if she had not mentioned you, considering that we went over to Hampstead to see you, and were much disappointed to find you had already retired to bed. You want shaking up, old fellow, that's what it is. You've been worrying yourself over this big business too

much. Your late partner's death has thrown
too much responsibility upon your shoulders.
How I wish I were not such a fool, and
could help you a little. But now that I
have returned, you must come out more,
Henry. It is quite time you came back to
the world. It is—let me see!—quite nine
months or more, surely, since that poor girl
met with her death—'

'Stop! stop!' cried Henry suddenly.
'What poor girl? What are you talking
about?'

Arthur looked bewildered.

'Why! Miss Crampton, or rather Mrs
Walcheren, of course. It was her death,
wasn't it, that led to the other. You must
have felt it terribly. Such a sudden shock,
and when you regarded her as almost one
of the family.'

'Oh! no, I didn't,' replied Hindes, in an
incoherent manner. 'Why should I have
felt it? She was nothing to me. I didn't
care about her. Why, to hear you talk in
that extravagant way,' he continued, turning
his suspicious eyes upon his brother, ' one

would think—one would almost imagine that I had had something to do with it all.'

'Something to do with it,' repeated Arthur, in a distressed tone of voice. 'Oh, Henry! how can you say such a thing! But you felt it deeply, I am sure. Anyone could see that from your altered appearance. But, my dear brother, there is such a thing, you know, as giving way too much to our feelings. You have lost two of your dearest friends, but you have your wife and children left. You must think of them, Henry, and also a little of me, of whom you are the last surviving relative. For all our sakes, dear old chap, try and rouse yourself from this morbid condition. A little amusement and gaiety will do you good. Hannah should have urged you to go out again before this. But, now that I have come home, I mean to persuade you to it, for my own sake as well as yours. Will you?'

'Of course I will,' replied Henry, sitting upright in his chair, and trying to look as if there were nothing the matter with him;

'we will go out together, Arthur, and have some larks as we used to do. I'm as fit as a fiddle. It's only Hannah who will have it I'm ill. Women are such coddles. But, now you are come, it will be all right. Let's make a night of it. Where shall we go? Tivoli first, and a little supper at Gatti's afterwards. Will that suit you, Artie? By Jove! the very sight of you has done me good.'

'I'd rather go to the theatre to-night, Henry. I shouldn't like to leave my little woman at home by herself, the first evening she spends in England. We will do the music-halls afterwards. What do you say to this? Come straight to Haxells' from the office, and dine with us. I will wire for Hannah to join us, and we'll make a party to the Lyceum in the evening. I can go now and secure a box. Will you do it, Henry? Do say yes!'

'Of course I'll do it, Arthur. What has my wife been telling you—that I'm not able to go to theatres and places of that sort? It's lies, I tell you—all lies. I'm

as fit as they're made.   All right, Bloxam.
I'll attend to you in a minute.'

'I'd better go now, Henry, and leave
you to your work,' said Captain Hindes,
with a perplexed face, 'you'll get on better
without me.   Don't forget.   Haxells' at
five, and we'll dine there, and spend the
evening at the theatre.   And I'll telegraph
to your wife at once that she may make
no engagement for to-night.   Good-bye
for the present, dear old fellow.   I'm
awfully glad to have met you again Hal.
Good-bye till this evening.'

But though he had said he was awfully
glad, Captain Hindes looked awfully sad
as he took his way back to the hotel to
tell his wife of his interview with his
brother.   He fulfilled his engagements,
secured a box at the theatre, sent Hannah
an invitation by wire, and ordered a good
dinner to be ready for the party at six.

But Hannah came, and the dinner came,
yet there was no appearance of Henry
Hindes.   After some delay, Arthur volun-
teered to go back to the City and see if he

had yet left the office. On reaching it, he was told that the 'governor' had been gone some time, and the clerk, who carried his papers to the hansom, had heard him distinctly give the order to drive to Hampstead, so the only thing his brother could do, was to jump into another hansom and follow him there. He expected to find Henry had mistaken the time of meeting, or had returned home to dress for the theatre, which, he had told him, was unnecessary. The man who opened the door of The Old Hall looked so surprised to see him, that Arthur's first inquiry was,—

'Has not your master returned?'

'Yes, sir, he has been home the best part of an hour.'

'Where is he?'

'In the library, I think, sir.'

Captain Hindes did not wait to be announced, but hastened to the library by himself. He found his brother seated in an arm-chair doing nothing, with his hands folded on his lap.

'Hullo!' cried Arthur.

Henry started as if he had been shot, and exclaimed,—

'Good God!' Then, turning towards the intruder, said angrily. 'How dare you startle me in that way? I have told you again and again—'

'Hal! Hal! it is I—Arthur,' replied the captain, quickly.

Henry Hindes turned a lack-lustre eye upon him, and said in a tone of surprise,—

'Arthur? but where have you come from? Why didn't you let me know you were coming home? We should have sent the carriage or something to meet you.

'Henry, old boy, what are you talking of?' said Captain Hindes. 'Why, I saw you at the office this morning, and you promised to dine with us this evening, and go to the theatre afterwards? Your wife is already in town, and I have come to see why you have not joined us. Had you forgotten your engagement? Why did you not come straight to Haxells', as you promised?'

'Did I promise?' asked his brother in a

stupid way. 'I suppose I have forgotten it! I have so much business to think of. But I had better tell Hannah I am going with you, or she will wait dinner for me.'

'I left Hannah with Edith, Hal, and the sooner we join them the better. I have my cab at the door, so come at once, like a good fellow,' said Arthur Hindes, who was beginning to feel seriously uneasy about his brother.

He persuaded him to accompany him back to town, however, and in another half-hour they had all sat down to dinner. Captain Hindes marked the anxious look in his sister-in-law's eye, as he related how he had found his brother; · but Henry picked up considerably during dinner, and even attempted some feeble attempts towards jocularity, which were accompanied, however, by such a silly, cackling laugh, that his wife's cheeks burned with shame to listen to him, and Arthur tried by all means in his power to cover his shortcomings by talking a great deal more nonsense than was his wont.

'I am sorry,' he said, as they started for the theatre, 'that I was unable to procure a box at the Lyceum. Everything was booked there for three weeks in advance, but I got seats at another theatre, which I daresay will prove just as amusing.'

'I shall like anything, naturally,' replied Edith; 'but you, Hannah, see so many pieces, I suppose, that you may be fastidious.'

'Indeed, you are mistaken,' said Hannah, with her quiet smile. 'Henry does not care, as a rule, to go out after dinner, and I cannot, of course, go without him. An evening at the theatre is almost as great a treat to me as to you, Edith.'

The theatre which Captain Hindes had selected was one of those which provide melodrama for the public amusement. There happened to be a very stirring piece on there at that moment, full of sensational scenes of murder, assault, and robbery. The murder was committed in the prologue, and the story dragged through three long acts afterwards, during which the assassin was being hunted down until he was finally brought to justice.

As soon as Hannah understood what they were likely to see, she became anxious and troubled on her husband's account, although she took great pains to conceal her feelings. The two ladies were seated in front of the box, whilst the gentlemen occupied the spaces behind their chairs. She could not, therefore, see her husband's face, but she sympathised with him all through the play. She fancied that the conversation between the brothers grew less and less as the piece proceeded, but that might be due to the fact that they had become interested in it. Her worst fears were, however, realised, when, as they were watching a scene in which the murderer betrayed himself to a woman, who had been on his track from the beginning, she suddenly heard Henry exclaim,—

'This is an insult! I will stand it no longer. I consider you had no right to bring my wife to see such a piece as this.'

Captain Hindes started to his feet at
once, the two ladies looked round in
amazement, and Hannah said, in an
agonised whisper,—

'Hush, Henry, hush, for Heaven's sake!
You will attract public notice. I am en-
joying the play immensely. Do sit down
and be quiet.'

'I will not sit down,' he continued,
loudly. 'I will not stay another moment
in this damned place. Here, Hannah, put
on your cloak and bonnet at once, and come
home with me. You sha'n't hear another
line of it.'

Hannah glanced at her brother and
sister-in-law with infinite distress, which
their looks returned, but, rising hastily,
she whispered to Arthur,—

'Don't make any fuss. Let me go
home with him. He is not well. Forgive me, Arthur; forgive us both, but
don't try to persuade him to stay.'

She threw her mantle over her shoulders
as she spoke, and, putting her hand through
her husband's arm, said gently,—

'Come, dear, I am quite ready to go home. Good-night, dear Arthur and Edie. Thanks so much,' and, with that, she drew him quickly away.

When they had disappeared, Captain and Mrs Hindes looked at each other in sorrowful surprise.

'What *is* the matter with him?' asked Edith of Arthur. 'Is he *mad*?'

'I am very much inclined to believe it,' replied her husband. 'There is certainly something very wrong about him, and I shall speak to a doctor on the subject to-morrow. Hannah says he has refused to see anybody, but, when a man begins to be as unreasonable as this, it is time his friends acted for him. I have not had time to tell you how I found him this afternoon, but I will when we get home.'

'I would rather return now if you have no objection, dearest,' said Mrs Hindes. 'This *contretemps* has taken away all my interest in the play. Poor Hannah! how I pity her.'

CHAPTER II.

HENRY and Arthur Hindes had been the
only children of their parents, and, as
young men, had been much attached to
each other; Arthur, perhaps, caring for
Henry more than Henry did for him, as
he joined admiration of his elder brother's
abilities and address to his affection. His
principal thought in coming home had been
the meeting with Henry again, and the
reality proved a bitter disappointment to
him. He lay awake half the night trying
to find some reason for his brother's un-
accountable conduct, but was unable to
think of any illness, except that of the
brain, that could make him behave in so
extraordinary a manner.

He determined, therefore, that, whether
Henry liked it or not, it was his duty to

consult a specialist on his behalf, and get
him, if possible, to pay him a visit. His
first action, therefore, in the morning was
to inquire for and gain an interview with
an eminent brain doctor, to whom he related, as well as he was able, all that had
occurred since his arrival in England.

The great man listened to him with
polite attention and in perfect silence. He
was a slender, delicate-looking man, with a
bald head, mild eyes and a pale complexion. No novice, to look at him,
would have imagined that that quiet eye
of his had the power to quell the ravings
of the greatest lunatic who ever tried to
dash his keeper's brains out. But, as he
sat quietly with clasped hands and gazed
at him, Captain Hindes felt his influence
without inviting it.

'A sad story, Captain Hindes,' he said,
when Arthur had finished; 'and it may be
you have guessed the truth. But no
disease is so subtle as that of the brain,
and I can give no opinion without seeing
your brother.'

'I am so afraid he would not admit you,' replied Arthur. 'His wife tells me he has such an abhorrence (forgive the term) of all medical men. But someone *must* see him. I feel sure of that.'

'Could you not introduce me as a friend of your own? Under any circumstances, you could not tell him who I am. It would defeat my efforts. I must observe him quietly and by myself,' said Doctor Govan.

'He is so morose and apparently averse to any company,' replied Arthur. 'I suppose you could not manage to see him at his office on pretence of doing business?'

'No, I'm afraid I should not play the *rôle* of a business man sufficiently well to escape detection. But, if you approve of the plan, I might pay him a visit at his own house some evening, in company with yourself, and be introduced as a fellow-passenger of yours from India, I have travelled in the East, so am equal to the occasion. Only give me half-an-hour in which to observe him at my leisure in his

own home, and I shall be able to satisfy
you if your surmises are correct or not.'

'Very good,' replied Captain Hindes.
'What evening will suit you, doctor?'

'I can go to-night, if you are sure
your brother will be at home.'

'I will wire to my sister-in-law, and let
you know the result at once.'

'Very well, sir. I will hold the time
at your disposal for, say, the next hour.'

Arthur thanked him, and withdrew to the
nearest telegraph office, whence he sent a
wire to Hannah, waiting there till he had
received her reply. It was satisfactory.

'We shall be at home this evening, and
glad to see you.'

With this, Arthur hastened back to
Doctor Govan, and received his promise
to meet him at the entrance of The Old
Hall gates at eight o'clock that night.
They were both punctual, and walked up
the drive together. The servant admitted
them to the library, where his master and

mistress usually spent their evenings, and they found Hannah sitting at her needle-work by the lamplight, whilst her husband lounged in a chair with a newspaper on his knees, but apparently doing nothing.

'Well, Hal!' exclaimed Arthur, cheer-fully, after he had saluted his sister-in-law, 'how are you? I should have looked you up before this, but I have been occupied half the day with a friend and fellow-passenger of mine, Doctor Govan. Let me make you known to one another. Doctor, this is my brother, Mr Hindes.'

As Hannah heard the profession of the stranger mentioned, she threw a quick glance towards Henry, to see how he would take it, but seemingly he had for-gotten the breach of good manners of which he had been guilty the night before, and re-covered his good temper, for he welcomed both his brother and his friend heartily.

'Delighted to see you both,' he said. 'Hannah, my dear, ring for brandy and soda. My wife says I behaved like a bear last night, Artie, in breaking up your

party so soon; but I was confoundedly
sleepy, old chap, and that's a fact, so you
must forgive me.'

'Why, Hal, I don't think you need
begin making excuses to me at this time
of day,' replied his brother, who looked at
the doctor, nevertheless, to see how he took
this very brief mention of a great insult.

But Doctor Govan's face was imperturb-
able, and no index to his feelings. He
accepted a glass of brandy-and-soda, and
entered into a pleasant conversation with
Henry Hindes respecting his business and
shipping prospects, whilst Arthur main-
tained small talk with Hannah. At last a
diversion was effected by the sound of a
child's whimpering outside.

'Wally being carried off to bed,' said
his mother, smiling. 'He is a very spoilt
boy, I am sorry to say, and it is seldom
effected without a controversy.'

'Wally,' cried his uncle. 'Oh, do have
him in, Hannah! You forget I have not
been introduced to my nephew yet.'

'It is so late,' she said, demurringly,

as she glanced at the clock, 'eight o'clock.
He ought to have been in bed half an
hour ago. And he may worry Doctor
Govan.'

'I'm sure he won't,' replied Arthur, as
he sprang towards the door; 'here, nurse,
bring that youngster this way. His mamma
wants him,' he continued, and in another
minute the little fellow ran into the room
and hid his face in his mother's lap.

It was evident how his father loved
him. Henry Hindes's features lighted up
with paternal affection as his little son
appeared, and he called the child to him
and placed him on his knee, that all the
room might admire him. Master Wally
was really a splendid specimen of a boy,
notwithstanding his plainness, with his head
of thick, curly hair, his large, dark eyes,
and dimpled neck and shoulders showing
above his embroidered frock.

'This is not a bad specimen to carry
on the family of the Hindes, eh, Arthur?'
inquired his father, proudly, as he passed
his hand over the infant's curls.

'He is a magnificent boy,' said his brother, enthusiastically, 'and I don't wonder you are proud of him, Henry. Why, he would make two of our little Charlie! And how fat he is! He must weigh about fifty pounds.'

'And he is really very intelligent for such a baby,' interposed Hannah; 'he has taught himself all his letters from his picture alphabet, and draws wonderfully for so young a child.'

'Yes,' added Henry Hindes, proudly, 'we are not at all ashamed of our son and heir. We consider he is as good as most.'

'I don't remember ever to have seen a finer child,' said Doctor Govan, willing to add his meed of admiration for the parents' pleasure, 'but you must be careful how you press so active a brain. Never forget that the body and the brain cannot grow together, unless at the expense of one or the other. Let him do nothing but play now! Half a dozen years hence will be plenty of time to begin cramming him. If the true history of most

murderers could be traced back, it would
be found that their brains had been unduly
charged when young, and broken down, or
become abnormal under the process. You
don't want this little man to develop into
a criminal, I'm sure,' said the doctor, as he
kindly patted the boy's shoulder.

But Henry Hindes's manner had completely changed. He snatched the child
from the stranger's reach, and rose majestic-
ally from his seat.

'What do you mean?' he demanded,
' by coupling my child's name with that of a
murderer? Have you come here to insult
me? I will not let you touch him again.
I never heard of such a thing in my life!
Perhaps you are a murderer yourself, since
it comes so pat to you to talk of them.
Leave my house at once! I will not have
my children's ears contaminated by hearing of such things!'

' Henry! Henry!' pleaded his wife, 'what
are you saying? This gentleman is our
guest—a friend of Arthur's. You must not
speak to him like that! You can't be well!'

'Not well!' he exclaimed vehemently, 'that's what you're always cramming down my throat nowadays. What is there about me that is not well? I suppose you want to get rid of me, and hope, by always dinning the lie, that I'm not well, into my ears, that you'll frighten me into dying. But you're mistaken! I'll live in spite of you! And is this the reason,' he continued, turning fiercely upon Arthur, 'that you brought this man to my house? You know I hate doctors. I told you yesterday that I don't believe in them. Why is he here? Tell me the truth at once!'

'There is nothing to tell, Henry,' replied his brother, in a tone of vexation, 'except that, since you choose to behave so unlike a gentleman, it will be the last time my friends ever intrude on you. I thought, in bringing Doctor Govan to my brother's house, that I was ensuring him the treatment due to his name and profession, but I see I was mistaken. We will not stay to be affronted any longer, so I will bid you good-night.'

He was turning away, wounded and unhappy, as he spoke, when a yell from little Wally arrested his footsteps. Henry, in his excitement, had dropped the child heedlessly on the carpet, where it lay screaming, whilst its father rubbed his hand in a bewildered manner through his hair. Hannah rushed to her baby and picked it up.

'That is always the way,' she said, indignantly, as she soothed the boy. 'He pretends to be so fond and proud of Wally, and yet, at the slightest provocation, he hurts or frightens him. That is why I did not wish to have him down, Arthur,' she whispered to her brother-in-law; 'I never bring him in contact with his father, if I can help it.'

'I am so sorry. I did not know,' said Arthur, with a look of commiseration. 'Come, Doctor Govan, I think we have been here long enough.'

'Yes, my object is effected,' returned the doctor, as he followed him out of the room.

Hannah ran off, at the same moment,

with her child to the nursery, and Henry
Hindes was left standing in the library
alone.   Captain Hindes did not speak
until they were clear of The Old Hall and
its surroundings, and then, as he and the
doctor were finding their way back to the
railway station, his tongue was loosed.

'Well, doctor?' he said, interrogatively,
'I suppose, after what has happened, that
you have no doubt of the case.'

'Not the slightest, my dear sir! Your
brother is no more mad that you are!'

Arthur turned round short, and regarded
him with astonishment.

'Not mad?' he ejaculated. 'Then what
makes him behave in so extraordinary a
manner?'

'That I cannot tell you. There may be
a dozen causes for it. I went there simply
to satisfy you with regard to danger to his
brain. Well, as far as I can see at present,
there is none! He has recourse to stimulant of some sort or another. It may be
spirits, or it may be a narcotic, which has
shattered his nerves and weakened his con-

trol over himself. But he is not mad ; you
may rest assured of that ; nor do I think
he will ever go mad. The brain is more
stupefied than excited.'

'But what, then, makes him behave so
strangely ? Doctor, if you will believe me,
my brother was one of the most pleasant-
mannered men about town. He was always scrupulously well-dressed, and had all
the bearing and appearance of a courtier.
He was remarkable for it, being a business
man. Now, he is rude, uncertain and
slovenly. He seems to have lost his
memory, too, and his business habits are, I
am told, falling off. What can be the
reason ?'

'Drink, my dear sir—you will excuse
my saying so, for I am not at all prepared
to say that Mr Hindes takes more liquor
than is good for him—but stimulant in
any shape, be it alcohol or morphia, will
have all the effect you describe on a man.
May I ask if your brother has experienced
any great shock lately, that may account
for his having recourse to sedatives ?'

'Well! about nine or ten months ago, his partner's daughter was killed by a fall, which so much affected her father that he died also a few weeks afterwards. Henry was a great friend of old Crampton's, and had known the girl from a child, so he naturally felt their loss, so did his wife, but hardly, I should imagine, to such a degree as to make him take to intemperate habits. Of course, it was a shock, because it happened so suddenly ; but our father died of heart disease—was well one hour, and dead the next—yet it did not affect my brother in this terrible fashion.'

'Has he had any trouble in business, Captain Hindes—any monetary losses ?'

'I am sure not. On the contrary, when Mr Crampton died, he left half his fortune, a very large one, to that little chap we saw this evening. I heard it was a stipulation that the money was to accumulate in the business till the boy comes of age. I should say my brother was never so well off, with regard to money, as he is at the present moment.'

'Well, of course these things are not
to be accounted for, unless one knows all
the inner workings of a man's mind,
but that Mr Hindes is in the habit of
taking more morphia than is good for him,
I am certain. *Why* he takes it, opens
up a different question! He has a very
powerful brain, and, naturally, a well regu-
lated one, and it must have taken a large
quantity of drugs, or he has indulged in
them for a considerable time, to bring him
to his present condition. I have said he
is not mad, and I repeat my dictum, but
I do not say that, if he continues his habits
of taking morphia (or some other drug as
deadly in its effects), that he will not
reduce his brain to the level of madness,
or a condition equally deplorable.'

'Good Heavens! how horrible!' cried
Arthur.

'You have sought my opinion, Captain
Hindes, and I have given you a faithful
one,' said Doctor Govan, as they parted
at the station; 'if you have your brother's
welfare at heart, wean him, if possible, from

this most pernicious habit, otherwise he will assuredly kill himself by it.'

Arthur Hindes returned to his hotel in the lowest spirits. He had never kept a secret from his wife, who was truly one with him in every sense of the word, so he told her all that had transpired between him and the doctor, and asked her what she would advise in the matter.

Edith thought for a moment, and then replied,—

'Since we have been talking about going into the country, Artie, wouldn't it be better if we went to Switzerland, or some mountainous district instead, and persuaded Henry and Hannah to accompany us? Away from London, and living under your own eye, you would be able to exert a better influence over him than here. Perhaps, then, you might, as the doctor said, wean your brother from this dreadful habit. I am sure poor Hannah is unhappy about it. The tears were standing in her eyes several times at the theatre last evening.'

' How can she be otherwise than miserable to see such a change in him? But have you calculated, my darling, what your proposal will entail on you? To live in the same house, for months, perhaps, with a man who may be as obnoxious to you as a drunkard. For this craving for morphia is very like drunkenness in its effects. It renders a man irresponsible for his actions, and may be the occasion of many unpleasant scenes between us. Am I justified in exposing you and the children to such things?'

' He is your only brother, Arthur, and you love him. That is enough for me. Were the consequences to be twice as disagreeable, I would risk them for your sake. Do what you think right in the matter, and trust me to do all I can to second your efforts.'

' You're the dearest wife a man ever had,' replied her husband, kissing her pretty face, 'and I thank you very much. Your plan is an excellent one, if I can only get Hal to accede to it. He will make all sorts of excuses about the business, of course, but I will not leave him alone until he consents to take a change. If it were only for a few weeks, it would be better than nothing.'

'Artie, dear, take my advice and don't speak to Henry about it first. Go and see Hannah. She is a sensible woman, and you can tell her all the doctor said, and enlist her on your side. She loves her husband —I am sure of that—and will be delighted to second any plan that is for his benefit.'

'Yes, dear, you are right again. To gain Hannah's consent will be gaining another ally. We shall be three against one. Henry must yield to us then. I will go over and speak to her to-morrow morning. You have lifted a load off my mind, Edith. I feel as if we must succeed now.'

Accordingly, the following morning, as Hannah was sitting at home, with little Wally playing at her feet, her brother-in-law was announced. Her first thought was to make some excuse for her husband's behaviour of the night before.

'Oh, Arthur, I am glad to be able to speak to you alone,' she commenced. 'It shocked me that poor Henry was so irritable last evening. Your friend must have thought he was insane. But that is the worst part about his illness. You can never be certain of him for ten minutes together. What did Doctor Govan think of such an outburst? What did he say?'

'He didn't say much, Hannah. You see, he is a medical man and used to such things.'

'But it made me feel so ashamed,' continued the wife, with the suspicious moisture in her eyes, 'and I hope you will not think me ungracious, Arthur, if I ask you not to bring any more of your friends here without giving us notice. Henry had been irritable all the afternoon, and if I had known a stranger was coming, I should have coaxed him to go to bed before you arrived.'

'I am very glad you didn't, Hannah, for I am going to tell you a secret. Doctor Govan is no friend of mine. I never set

eyes on him till yesterday morning. I
brought him here expressly that he should
see Henry in his own home, and be able
to report on his health, without his being
aware he was examined by an expert.'

'An expert!' exclaimed Hannah, paling.
'What do you mean?'

'A specialist, then, if you prefer the term
—anyway, a medical man who is at the top
of the tree.'

'But why — why?' she said, with a
startled gaze.

'Because I felt very much alarmed about
his condition. His conduct at the theatre
the other night, joined to his altered manners and appearance, all combined to make
me think that he must have had some shock
to addle his brain. Hannah, don't be angry,
but Henry has behaved to me, ever since I
came home, like nothing short of a madman,
and it made me very uneasy about him.'

'And was—this—this gentleman a mad
doctor, and did you bring him here to examine my husband?' she inquired with
surprise.

'He was; and I certainly brought him here that he might give me a truthful report on Henry's condition,' replied Captain Hindes.

'How dared you?—how dared you?' she panted.

'Why, Hannah, I never thought you would take it like this! I consider that you have somewhat neglected your duty, in not having called in a doctor to him long ago. I think my brother is in a very critical state. Doctor Govan does not, I am glad to say, consider him mad, but he says he will drive himself so if he is not carefully watched in the future. He pronounces him to be suffering from the effects of opium, or some other narcotic, and that he has weakened his brain by its use, and is hardly responsible for his actions. Henry is my brother, you must remember, Hannah, as well as your husband, and it is my duty to look after him. Doctor Govan says that, if we cannot wean him from the habit he has fallen into, he will inevitably kill himself by it. Now, Edith and I have been talking the matter over, and came to the conclusion that we must all act in concert. I am willing to take my wife and family to Switzerland, or any distant place we may agree upon, if you and Henry will join us there, so that I may have him under my own eye, and do my best to restore him to health. You will do your part, I am sure, Hannah, and persuade your husband to consent to this arrangement.'

'*I will not!*' replied Hannah, with closed lips.

CHAPTER III.

ARTHUR looked at her in amazement. Was this his gentle sister-in-law? Her very voice seemed changed, and her frame was shaking with her unusual emotion.

'What do you mean?' he asked. 'Surely you have Henry's welfare at heart as much as we have.'

'I think I have, Arthur; but I will not attempt to persuade him to go to Switzerland, or any other place, unless it should be alone with me. I have already told you that he cannot bear the noise of children, even that of his own, neither does he care for company. I was sorry and surprised that, knowing his state of health, you should have introduced a stranger at The Old Hall without giving us notice, but now that I find he was a mad doctor, brought here to examine my husband without my leave or cognisance, I think it little short of an insult.'

'An insult? Oh! Hannah! that is too hard a word,' interposed her brother-in-law.

'I don't say you meant it so, but at the least it was a piece of great officiousness on your part. How dared you think, or let others think,' she went on, suddenly flaring up, 'that my husband—is *mad?* Is that brotherly solicitude? For shame! For shame! Had I known who your *friend* was, I would have turned him from my door.'

'Then there is no chance, I suppose,' said Arthur, sorrowfully, 'of persuading you to join your forces to ours, and inducing Henry to go away with us for a change?'

'Not the slightest. He does not need change. If he does, we will go away quietly together. Don't think me unkind, Arthur, but I have already told you what Henry's illness arises from. I know he sometimes takes a little dose of morphia, or smokes a pipe of opium; he does it to allay the pain of neuralgia, which often unfits him for business; many other neuralgic patients do the same. The pain he endures unfits him for society also; it upsets his nerves and makes him irritable. But to call him mad—to bring a mad doctor to see him, without asking his consent, or mine— Oh! it was cruel—cruel!'

She turned her back upon her brother-in-law, and went on with her work, whilst he sat there, hardly knowing what to do or say.

'How am I to persuade you, Hannah,' he resumed at last, 'that I acted in all love and kindness towards my brother and you? I believed that, living always by his side, you could not have noticed what is so very palpable to me—the extraordinary change in poor Henry—'

'Not seen it?' she interrupted him with. 'Not wept over it, and prayed over it for months past! Why not say at once that

I do not love my husband, Arthur? I
know far more of him than you do, and
could have saved you the trouble of bringing a *mad* doctor to gloat upon his infir-
mities. Henry is unhappy, poor darling!
He has been unhappy ever since his
partner's death, and his nerves have
become unstrung. He is foolish, perhaps,
to take so much morphia, but it soothes
and relieves him, and anything is better
than that he should suffer. But you will
not cure him—neither you nor your
doctors! Only time and affection will
do that, with perfect quiet. I will not,
therefore, have him disturbed, nor worried in any way, either by relations or
strangers. I will not let him go to
public amusements again, which only tire
him, but he shall stay at home with
me till God, in His own good time, sees
fit to cure him of his complaint.'

'Forgive me, Hannah,' said Captain
Hindes, after a pause, 'I daresay I have
been very officious, but I did it for the
best. Won't you believe that?'

'Yes, I believe that.'

'And I will leave Henry for the future to you. But, oh! do try to wean him from that dreadful habit. And look here, my dear, under these circumstances, what is the use of my remaining in London? I cannot afford the expense of an hotel, and came here, as you must know, only to be near you and Henry. But it can be no pleasure to me to continue to see him in this condition, especially if I can do him no good. It unnerves me, Hannah. He is a wreck of his former self. We shall only quarrel if we continue to meet, so the sooner I take my wife and little ones into the fresh country, the better. Don't be surprised, then, if we start almost immediately, but I shall, of course, run up and say good-bye to you and Henry before we go.'

He held out his hand to her as he spoke, but, to his surprise, instead of taking it, Hannah covered her face with her own, and burst into a flood of tears.

'Oh! it is so hard—so hard,' she sobbed,

'to see him so unlike himself, and find no remedy on any side. I would—I would,' she continued hysterically, 'give my life to see him as he used to be. But it is in vain wishing for it—all in vain—in vain!'

Arthur sat down beside her again, and took her hand.

'My dear Hannah,' he said, 'I feel sure that all the dear old man wants is a complete change. He has been brooding over these sad deaths of the Cramptons, and that, added to business matters being a great anxiety, and this confounded neuralgia driving him half crazy, has had a great effect upon his mind. But, if he went right away, it would work a miracle for him. Come, dear girl, think over my proposal a second time, and bring him to Switzerland, with Edie and me.'

'No, no, no; anything but that,' said Hannah, shaking her head. 'I will pray for him, and strive for him at home, but he must not go into society. Oh, Arthur, cease worrying me about it! I am so miserable—so miserable.'

'My poor sister, I can see you are. Well, as you say, we must trust him to God.   Good-bye for the present.   Edie shall give you proper notice of our next visit.   But this isn't as it used to be—eh, Hannah?'

'No; nothing is as it used to be,' she responded, as she wished him farewell.

As soon as her brother-in-law was out of sight and hearing, poor Hannah gave vent to her tears in right earnest.   How was all this to end, she thought.   What would become of her hapless husband if it went on much longer?   His condition had already attracted public notice.   The next thing would be that he was declared unfit to conduct his business, and their affairs would have to be handed over to the care of a stranger.   She foresaw nothing in the future but misery for herself and her children.   She saw no prospect of ever having her daughters to live at home, for every day strengthened her resolve not to bring them in contact with so depraved and uncertain a father.   Nothing remained for her but a life of servitude and loneliness, while she pandered to a sin she abhorred for the sake of the children she loved. Even so innocent a pleasure as the society of her brother and sister-in-law was denied her. Henry's conduct had estranged them. Little by little, she foresaw she would be called upon to relinquish everything that had made her existence pleasant to her.

When her husband returned home and she communicated the fact of his brother's proposed departure to him, he became as angry as if he had been doing everything in his power to make their stay in town agreeable. He called Arthur ungrateful, and Edith a fool, and wanted to know why they had ever returned to England if they intended to spend their furlough apart from the only relations they had in the world.

'I think you forget, Henry,' interposed his wife, 'that Arthur is not very rich, and to live in London with five children is rather expensive work. Their weekly bills must amount to something

terrific.   I don't wonder at his being
anxious to get them all off into the
country.   He talks of going to Switzerland.'

'Switzerland! Bosh!' exclaimed Henry
Hindes.   'Why don't he bring the lot of
them to The Old Hall?   There's plenty
of room for them here!   I should like
to see the children running about!   The
place has been infernally dull since you
sent the girls away.   Just write and tell
Arthur that the old place is at his disposal whenever he likes.   Why didn't
they come here from the beginning?
What was the obstacle?'

'*You* were, Henry!' said Hannah,
looking at him steadily.   'Have you
forgotten that already?'

The man shivered, and turned away.
But, the next moment, he was braving it
out.

'*You* were, you mean, confound you!'
he retorted.   'But if I choose to have my
brother here, I shall do so without asking
your leave, and that I tell you.'

'I don't think he would care to accept your invitation now,' she said, 'for you have behaved so rudely to him—once at the theatre and yesterday, when his friend was present,—that he would, I fancy, be rather afraid of subjecting himself to the daily risk of renewing such scenes. Arthur told me this afternoon that—'

'What?—what?' cried Hindes, quickly, 'what did he tell you? He doesn't suspect, does he, Hannah—he doesn't think —you haven't *told* him,' he continued, grasping her arm as if he held it in a vice. 'You haven't betrayed me—speak, speak, for God's sake! Don't keep me in suspense!'

He looked so abject as he put the question with trembling eagerness, that her heart went out to him with a great burst of pity. He was a murderer—but she loved him.

'No, no, darling!' she replied, with unwonted tenderness, as she bent down and kissed his haggard face, 'how can you think so for a moment? I shall never,

never betray you, Harry ; not even at the
bar of Heaven.   If I am brought up there
as witness against you, I will go to hell
sooner than open my mouth.   Don't think
it of me!   You are not safer with God
Himself than you are with me, my poor
Harry!'

'I know it, I know it!' he muttered ;
'but why can't Arthur come here, then?'

'Because—oh! there are many reasons ;
don't make me reiterate them.   But one is,
that I am afraid your conduct would ex-
cite his attention and, perhaps, his suspicions.   You are not master of yourself,
Henry!   That dreadful morphia makes
you just the same as if you were intoxi-
cated.   It is killing you, body and soul.
You take far too much of it.   You must
give it up.   Oh! do promise me, Hal, to
try and do without it.   Half your time you
are so stupid, you don't know what you are
saying or doing.   Even the servants see
the alteration in you.   *Do* give it up,
Henry.   I would ask it of you on my
bended knees if I thought it would have

any effect. Promise me you will throw
the horrid bottle away, and never take any
more of it.'

' I cannot, I cannot!' he replied in a
despairing whisper. ' I take it to keep *her*
away. Directly I leave it off for a night
she comes and reproaches me with—
you know what—and I cannot bear her
eyes, they drive me mad.'

' Dear husband, it is only your fancy.
She is far too happy, by this time, not
to have forgotten and forgiven long ago.
Only pray for God's forgiveness and all
will be right. Or come away with me, as
you proposed once before, and let us try to
be at peace with our children again, in a
new land.'

' Not now,' he said, shaking his head,
'not while Arthur is in England. He
would suspect—he would come too. Wait!
—wait, till he is gone away again.'

' Oh! Harry, never mind him. He may
not go back to India for years. And your
health is getting worse and worse. New
scenes and interests would drive these

feverish fancies out of your head. What is anything worth, in comparison to that? Leave the business to take care of itself! Sell it for anything it may fetch ; only come away from England, and let me try to help you to overcome the dreadful habit you have contracted.'

'It is too late, my dear.   I could not do without it now.   I should go mad.'

'Henry, you *will* go mad if you do not leave it off! That Doctor Govan, who came here last evening, detected your fondness for morphia at once, and he told Arthur—'

But the idea that he was watched, raised the devil in Henry Hindes at once.

'How *dare* Arthur set traps to catch me?' he exclaimed furiously, 'and you are aiding and abetting him. *Who* told you what the doctor said? When have you seen my brother since? Are you all in league against me?'

'No! no! Henry ; don't be so foolish,' replied his wife. 'No one says or thinks anything except for your good.   But your

brother is anxious on your account. Anyone would be who had known you in
former days. You cannot know how ill
you look. And so he brought his friend
to see you, hoping he might suggest a
remedy. But Doctor Govan said nothing
will do you any good until you leave off
morphia.'

'D—n his impudence!' exclaimed
Hindes, angrily; 'that's what he was
sneaking round here for, was it? I'll teach
him to lay siege to me in my own house.
The next time he shows his face here, I'l
kick him out, and Arthur into the bargain.
But it's all your fault,' he continued, turning round upon her. 'If you didn't go
about with that long face of yours, people
wouldn't be trying to find out what was
the matter with me. Sending the children
away from home, too ; why, that in itself is
enough to raise any one's suspicion—you,
who always advocated home education,
especially for girls. It is abominable—in-
famous—that a man cannot have any
dependence even on his wife!'

The injustice of this attack, coming so immediately upon her kindness to him, stirred all the resentment of which she was capable in Hannah's breast.

'You are unjust to me,' she cried, 'most unjust! What other woman would have done for you what I have done? What other woman would have stayed by your side, after she knew what *I* know? I sent the girls away because I felt it was impossible they should be brought up in the same house with you, and the sequel has proved I was right. If any suspicions have been aroused, it is by your own conduct. The fatal habit you have contracted is as bad as that of drinking. It deprives a man of all self-respect—all forethought—all control over himself, or his temper. The scenes which took place in the theatre, and here, last night, are horrible to me and degrading to yourself. I have offered to exile myself with you in order to help you fight against the demon that possesses you, and you have refused. I can do no more. Henceforward, you must go your own way, without aid from me! I can only wait and watch for the end.'

She turned from him indignantly as she concluded, and Henry Hindes felt for the first time as if he were indeed deserted by God and man.

The idea rendered him frantic. He dashed out of the room and stumbled upstairs. At the top he met little Wally coming to bid papa and mamma good-night, carefully feeling his way down the broad stairs by holding on tight to the banisters. Master Wally was, as his nurse said, 'quite a man.' He highly objected to being led, or held by the hand. 'Let Wally go, all by his self,' he would say, and so, clad in his white frock and blue ribbons, he was laboriously making his way downwards, whilst his nurse followed, smiling proudly at his independence.

Just as he had commenced to descend the last flight, he encountered his father, mad with rage and fear and morphia. He did not even seem to see the little figure he so dearly loved, as he stumbled upstairs, and half fell, half brushed rudely against it. The baby lost his slight hold of the railings at once, and fell to the very bottom, where he lay motionless.

A shriek from the nurse brought Hannah quickly out of the library, when she found her little son lying on the mat in the hall. As she raised him, she glanced upwards and saw her husband standing at the head of the staircase, paralysed with fright. She had only time to ask, 'Is this *your* doing?' when he threw his arms wildly above his head, and exclaiming, 'The cliffs! the cliffs! A judgment! a judgment!' rushed away and locked himself into his own room.

Hannah had no care, at that moment, but for her little child. The nurse was sobbingly informing her how the dear baby was coming downstairs so beautifully, and how the master fell against him and upset his balance, and she hoped her mistress wouldn't fancy it was by any fault of hers, when Hannah interrupted her by saying,—

'Go and tell James to fetch Doctor Sewell at once, Annie, and I will lay Wally on the library sofa.'

She carried her little son away as she spoke, and sat down with him in her arms. Wally had not yet given any signs of consciousness, but lay like a bruised lily on his mother's lap. His face was very white, and his eyes were closed, but there was no appearance of his having sustained any injury. But when Dr Sewell arrived, he looked very serious over the misadventure. He measured the height of the fall, and examined the child's head and temples carefully. Then he said, as Wally stirred and moaned, and gave signs of returning consciousness,—

'You had better put the little fellow to bed, Mrs Hindes, and let his nurse sit up with him during the night. I will send a draught for him to take, and will be here early to-morrow.'

'But, doctor,' said Hannah, anxiously, 'you don't think this fall will have any bad effects, do you? He has so often tumbled about before.'

'Of course, of course,' replied the doctor, cheerfully, 'and will do so again, no doubt, but there is no harm in taking a little precaution. He is getting a heavy boy now, you know, and a fall is, consequently, more risky. But, doubtless, he will be all right after a few days' rest. Get him to bed, and don't take him out again till I have seen him in the morning.'

He left her with this sorry bit of comfort, and she carried her little boy up to her own bed, and prepared to watch by him for the night herself. As long as the nurse attended on her and Wally, she was undisturbed, but when she had dismissed her, and all the house was quiet, she heard the door between her room and that of her husband softly unclose, and Henry Hindes's haggard face appeared in the opening. Hannah felt so much disgust for him at that moment, that she could not help showing the feeling in her face and manner.

'Oh, go away, go away!' she exclaimed with averted eyes, 'I can't bear to see you or hear your voice. You have done enough mischief, God knows! Go away and leave me in peace with my child. It is the least thing you can do.'

'Is he dead?' demanded Hindes, in an awed whisper.

'He is not; but it is not your fault that he still lives. And what terrible results may follow this unnatural fall, no one knows. I told you what your habits would lead to. You have the consolation of knowing that you have injured, and perhaps killed, your favourite child by your fatal indulgence.'

'No! not killed—not *killed*—' he repeated hoarsely, 'it is impossible. God cannot have so little mercy.'

'Mercy!' cried Hannah, shrilly, for the accident to her baby had dried up, for the time being, every drop of the milk of human kindness in her, 'what mercy have you a right to expect at His hand—*you*, who showed none? You are not satisfied with making *one* mother childless. You must try and take the only joy left in my wretched life from me. You deprived me of the society of my girls, and now you want to murder my boy.'

She had used the word inadvertently, but it stabbed the unfortunate man before her to the heart. He glared wildly at her for a minute, and then, with a low cry like the protest of a wounded animal, he slammed the door between them, and locked it on the other side. Hannah had a bolt on hers, and she rose at once and drew it. She felt she could not endure his presence again that night. So she sat by Wally's side, and watched his feverish slumbers alone till daylight.

CHAPTER IV.

DOCTOR SEWELL's report, the next morning, was not entirely satisfactory.

It was true that Wally was quite conscious, and had eaten a good breakfast, but he cried when he was moved, and did not seem to wish to get up, which was so far fortunate, because the medical man strictly forbade his doing so. But it made Hannah very uneasy, since it plainly denoted that he had sustained more injury than was outwardly apparent.

She did not see her husband all the day, during which he kept strictly to his own room, and she was glad of it, for she felt that she could not have spoken to him as she ought. She was already ashamed of her outburst of the day before, but did not feel as if she could speak much differently even now. For, as she sat by Wally's side, trying to soothe his fretfulness under pain, her thoughts would revert to sweet, beautiful Jenny, struck down through the same hand. Was this really a judgment on her husband for his unconfessed crime? Was *his* child to be taken from him, in the same way and by the same hand that had made other parents, as loving as himself, childless? But it was hard on her—very, very hard, that she should suffer, through her little son, for his father's sins. Hannah sat by the baby's side, thinking these sad thoughts throughout the day, and when night fell, and Wally was asleep, she wrestled with Heaven in prayer that the cup might pass away from her. Yet she knew, even while she prayed, that it is part of the world's plan that the innocent shall suffer for the guilty, and often more than they suffer themselves.

When the household was once more sunk in sleep, Hannah bethought her of her husband, of whom she had heard nothing since the previous night. What was he doing? Whom had he spoken to?

What had he had to eat? She felt she must ascertain these points before she went to rest herself, for the doctor had told her, since the boy was out of immediate danger, it must be days, perhaps weeks, before he could finally pronounce on the ultimate effects of the accident, and therefore it behoved her not to try her strength more than was absolutely needful. With the purpose of seeing her husband, she tried the door between them, but found it was still locked on his side, therefore she went round to that which opened into the passage, which he had left unfastened, and went softly in. The sight which met her eyes was a pitiable one. Henry Hindes was on his knees beside the bed, moaning in the agony of his spirit. Yet, such is the force of a mother's love, that the expression of his pain did not move her as it had done that evening in the library. For since then had he not injured *her* child, which had awakened a twofold repulsion in her breast against him; one for herself and the other for Mrs Crampton. Hannah had never realised till now what *her* agony of loss had been. As she approached him, Hindes lifted his blood-shot eyes and muttered,—

'Say it at once, for God's sake! Is he gone?'

'Wally? No!'

'Thank Heaven!'

'Don't be too quick to do that, Henry. He is in pain. There is no knowing what injuries he may not have sustained. Dr Sewell will give no opinion. He says time only can show; pray that God may have mercy upon us, and not visit your sins on the head of your unoffending child.'

Hindes groaned.

'What would the worst be—the worst that could happen to him?'

'Spinal disease. A cripple for life, or a lingering death,' replied Hannah, sternly

She could not find it in her heart to lighten the blow to the author of it.

'A cripple for life—a lingering death— my Wally, my darling Wally!' sobbed the father. 'Oh, Hannah, my punishment is heavier than I can bear.'

'You will *have to* bear it, if God wills; so shall I — as the Cramptons had to bear—'

'No, no, Hannah, for Heaven's sake, no!' screamed Henry Hindes, as he cowered beside the bedclothes. 'I have seen his face—Mr Crampton's face—before me ever since, saying, "*Now* you will know! *Now* you will know!" I drugged myself with morphia last night, but it was no good. He was there all the time—all the time.'

'This is your fancy, Henry. I have told you so before. It is your own thoughts that take bodily shape to haunt you. But this sad accident calls loudly for reparation and repentance. Confess your sins to God, Henry. Ask Him to forgive them — tell Him everything — your unhallowed wishes and desires, your hasty temper and revenge, your disregard of advice and entreaty. He knows all your weakness, and will have compassion on it, and, perhaps, for the sake of your penitence and desire of amendment, He may mercifully spare our little one, and avert the possible consequences of your muddled senses.'

' I *will* pray, I *will* repent,' moaned the unhappy man, with his face still hidden, ' and I will confess, Hannah, everything—everything—if God will only hear and forgive me.'

' He is sure to do that,' said Hannah, more kindly; 'though it is impossible to say in what way He may answer your prayers. But we will both pray, Henry, will we not, that this miserable affair may leave no bad effects behind it? And, should our prayers be granted, you will promise me to give up taking morphia, for the future, and keep your brain clear for the duties of every-day life. This would never have happened, remember, except that you were too stupefied, to see the child's danger, or that you were in his way.'

' I know, I know,' he answered, ' but he is better to-night, is he not?'

' There is no knowing—Doctor Sewell

says it is impossible to say,' she said, as she turned and left him to his own reflections.

Many more days passed in this miserable uncertainty. Doctor Sewell brought two more doctors with him, to make a thorough examination of the little child, but, though they all agreed that the spine had been injured, they could not decide to what extent. All they could say was, that Wally must be kept on his back till the real extent of the mischief was ascertained. It might be months, even years, before the matter was finally decided; meanwhile, he must be kept perfectly still while indoors, and only taken out in the air, lying flat on his back, in a wheeled chair. It was a pleasant prospect to have to keep a sturdy child of Wally's age amused from morn to night, whilst in a recumbent position; but it was the only chance for him, so it must be done. The poor mother sat down patiently to await the verdict, but Henry Hindes raved like a madman at the doctors' orders, and

declared he should shoot himself before
the best or worst was made known to him.
Hannah insisted that he should return to
his duties, and leave her to the melancholy
charge of looking after the child.

'You are worse than useless here,
Henry. In fact, your presence and loud
lamentations over him disturb Wally, and
make him fretful and restless. Besides,
you have your own duties to attend to, and
must neglect them no longer. If you are
sincere in your sorrow over this accident,
prove it by doing your duty like a man,
and attending the office as usual.'

For Henry Hindes had shut himself up
since the night he had thrown his child
down the stairs, and refused to meet
anybody, on business or otherwise. Mr
Abercorn, the chief clerk, and Mr Bloxam,
the cashier, had been up to Hampstead
together to inquire the reason of their
employer's non-appearance in the city, and
Mrs Hindes had been obliged to tell them
that her husband was confined to his room
and quite unfit to see them, or attend to

business for the present. She was obliged
to invent this fiction, for the reason that,
for some days, Hindes was imbibing opium
to such an extent, and raving of what
distressed his conscience so freely, that
she felt, at all hazards, she must keep
everybody from him but herself.

Captain Hindes and his wife came over,
as soon as they heard of poor Hannah's
fresh trouble, and would have done anything in their power to help her, but it was
a case where the assistance of one's fellow-
creatures could avail nothing, and the only
thing was to wait and hope. Arthur did
not see his brother on the occasion, for
Henry had shut himself up in his own room,
as usual, and refused to open the door.
He had come chiefly to tell Hannah that
they had found a little cottage to suit them
in the Isle of Wight, and intended moving
into it at once. She was not sorry to hear
their news. She longed to get them, and
everybody connected with her husband, out
of the way, so that she might have him to
herself, and shield him from all prying eyes

and ears. During his short period of
seclusion, she had carried all his meals to
his room with her own hands, and coaxed
him to eat them by every means in her
power. And, now that the first shock was
over, she ordered him to return to his
official duties as she would have ordered a
boy to return to school. He had reduced
himself to such a state that he was no longer
capable of regulating his actions. His re-
appearance in the office was so far bene-
ficial that a business never proceeds so well
and regularly as when the head of it is
absent; but Hindes had almost rendered
himself incapable, by this time, of taking any
active part in the management of affairs,
which he left entirely to his two chief men,
Abercorn and Bloxam, whilst he sat brooding in his private room, or wandered rest-
lessly about the streets, waiting for the
doctors' verdict respecting Wally, and
wondering how much longer they would
keep him in suspense. He consulted the
best known physicians about the child, and
brought the cleverest surgeons to see him,

but the answer of each one was the same,
'Wait, wait! This is a case for time. No
one can foretell the upshot of such a fall
until the child has, in a measure, done
growing.'

Done growing! And Wally was not yet
three years old. Henry Hindes would
groan within himself, and say that it was
impossible. He could not be kept so long
in suspense. He must know at once. He
almost felt sometimes as if he would rather
his boy had been killed outright, than condemned to such a lingering illness as this
promised to be. He could not bear it!
He could not! He could not!

During those days of mortification and
miserable impatience, how more than
vividly Jenny Crampton's fair image returned to his memory to torture him. His
wife had advised him to confess all his unhallowed desires and wishes regarding her,
but even Hannah knew little of what he
had hoped, in his maddest moments, regarding Jenny. She had been a flirt—no doubt
of that, though her errant heart had been

caught fast at last by Frederick Walcheren.
But before those days, when Henry Hindes
had had no reason to affront her by the expression of his jealousy, she had not dis-
dained to flirt a little with him on her own
account.

She had meant her expressions of
regard for him as nothing but a flash of
coquetry; but he, with his secret passion
for the beautiful girl, and the mad dreams
he sometimes indulged in concerning her,
had chosen to translate her kindness in
a far warmer manner than she intended
he should. And these tender moments,
which were seared upon his memory,
came back with irritating persistency to
him now that they were over for ever—
that even the remembrance of them had
been dispelled by the terrible knowledge
that his hand had quenched them for ever!

One day that he had brought her a
little souvenir for her birthday—merely
an *étui* of velvet, filled with scissors and
thimble, and the rest of the rubbish provided for the work of ladies who *don't*

work, mounted in gold, and encrusted with turquoises—Jenny had kissed him—had advanced her ripe, pouting lips of her own accord, and pressed them upon his. He could recall to this day how the piece of coquetry affected him. She had guessed, well enough, her power over this apparently staid, sensible man of business, and liked to show it. She had smiled on him the while in her saucy way and made his head swim. It was this circumstance, and one or two others like it, that had caused Jenny to turn against him and say hard things about him directly she had gained a lover whose heart she wished to keep. It was the remembrance of such things that had made her fear the expression of his jealousy, and declare he took an un-warrantable interest in her affairs.

Yet, the feeling her kiss had raised in his breast haunted the wretched man long after he had caused her death. Sometimes the one memory pained him more than the other. He would wonder, if he had been bold enough to speak openly to Jenny of his feelings regarding her, whether she would have listened to his story and requited his affection, just a little, in return. She would dance before him, like an airy phantom, all through the dull, old streets of the city, beckoning him, with her dimpled little hand, to come nearer and nearer, and taste her lips once more! And then, when he had worked his imagination up to a pitch of frenzy, the scene would change, and he would see, instead, Jenny lying still and white in her shroud, with the purple marks of foul decomposition upon her cheeks and brow. Yet, dead as she appeared, her wraith would still have the power to unclose its lustre less eyes and livid lips to say, ' *These* are the lips with which I kissed you, and *you* it was who rendered them like this, unfit for anyone but the worms to touch again.'

He would see her in the sunshine, and in the gloaming—in the crowded streets and by the deserted river-side—in the

Mart and in his private office—till he
nearly went mad with the longing to
stamp her out from his brain, or to plunge
himself into the silent river and follow
her wherever she might be.

Much as she had haunted and pursued
him since that fatal moment when he pushed
her over the Dover cliff, never had he seen
her as he had done since Wally's accident!
She seemed to come now with a mocking
smile upon her lips—a smile which said,
'*I* did it! *I* made him fall! *I* did for you
what you did for me! Who was it made
you drink morphia until you had paralysed
your brain? *I!* Who was it drove you
wild as you stumbled up these stairs? The
remembrance of *me!* You killed me, and
I have subjected your boy to a living death
—a death far worse than mine—a death
which will numb his nerves and his brain,
and keep him a prisoner for life, tied to a
sofa, inert in mind and muscle. Wally's
accident was due to me! *You* made my
parents childless. I have robbed you of
your son and heir.'

He suffered extra torture from the daily inquiries which met him as he entered the office. Of course, every clerk there had heard the story of his child's fall, and was anxious to learn what the effects might be. The constant question of, ' How is the little boy to-day, sir ? I trust he is better ; ' or, ' Have the doctors given any decided opinion about Master Wally, sir ? Is he any worse this morning ? ' drove the unfortunate father nearly out of his senses, and often caused him to swear, in a most unfatherly manner, in return for the kindly inquiries made on the child's behalf.

He could not banish the thought, even for a moment. His brother had migrated to the Isle of Wight, and he never saw his wife, except by Wally's bedside. The boy, too, who had been so strong and sturdy was fast being reduced, under the effect of inertion and confinement, to a thin and sickly-looking child. His hands, that used to be so chubby, had grown white and limp; his abundant hair had been cropped to make him more comfortable, and his temper was fractious and irritable. In fact, he was no longer the little Wally of whom he had been so proud. He was almost as much changed, for the worse, as Henry Hindes himself. Sometimes, as his father sighed the long days away, Hannah's admonition would recur to his mind: ' Confess your sins to God, Henry! Tell Him everything! He knows your weakness and will have compassion on it!'

But where should he confess? To whom could he pour out the tale of his sins and his follies? He could not trust a private person, and the parsons of the Protestant church, though they professed to hear the confessions of the dying, who were passing into the very Presence of the great Father-Confessor of us all, and had no need of any more ministrations of man, would not hear a word from the living and the strong, who were still battling with the difficulties of life. He recalled what Mr Bloxam had told him one day, not so long before, of the consolation Catholics found in confession, and how it relieved their souls and consciences to receive absolution from their priests. Hindes wondered how they set about it, whether it was a difficult task, or easily accomplished. In the course of the long walks he frequently took round the City, when his conscience would not let him sit still in the office any longer, he had often come across a little Roman Catholic church, in the East-end of London, where the congregation seemed of a poorer class than the generality. One afternoon he had peeped inside it, and looked, with wonder, at the brass ornaments and artificial flowers on the altar, at the dimly-lighted swinging lamp before the Virgin's shrine, at the confessional on either side the building, covered in dingy red cloth, with the name of the priest, who occupied it, in white letters over the portal.

Henry Hindes had tried to confess his sins to God. He had poured out his soul in prayer, as well as he knew how, but the words had sounded hollow and meaningless in his own ears. He did not know God. He had never been used to talk to

Him, and now that he had so great neces-
sity of His reply, he did not know how to
address Him. True, he had been a constant attendant at church, but the service
had been a mockery to him. He had
never really prayed from his heart. And
now his prayers seemed to come back
upon himself, unanswered, as if he had
uttered them to the empty air. Wally
grew no better for them. He still lay
in his mother's bed, weary, languid and
fretful. God had certainly not yet seen
fit to answer any prayers on his behalf.
Hindes wondered within himself if confession would really do any good—whether
he would feel easier after it—and whether
he should please Heaven by the effort,
and gain some good from it for Wally?
It was against all his preconceived ideas
of comfort or right, and he shrunk from
the notion with aversion. What person,
not brought up to the practice from childhood, does not? A priest will tell you
that therein lies the merit of the sacrifice,
but the sins that are usually confided to

the keeping of the confessional are very
innocent ones.   Few criminals take the
burden of their crimes there.   They are
either too hardened, or too fearful.   The
confessionals are, generally speaking, occupied by women, who bring the same list
of follies, week after week, to be absolved
from.   But that does not prove that there
are not plenty of heavier burdens lying
at the bottom of the lust of the eye and
the pride of life.

But Henry Hindes had had no experience of the confessional, either as a
vanity or a relief.   He knew what he had
heard concerning it, and he knew that, if
he entered it, it would be strictly incognito,
for he knew no Catholics, nor any priests.
One afternoon, when his sins were lying
on his mind, if possible, heavier than
usual, he saw the door of the little East-
end church standing invitingly open, and
walked in, and took a seat to rest himself.
The place was nearly empty.   Two or
three women, clad in sober black, and a
sprinkling of half-grown children, were the

only occupants, and they were all engaged
in prayer. There was a sense of drowsi-
ness and a subtle smell of incense about
the little temple of God that was con-
sonant with the man's perturbed feelings,
and seemed to pacify them. Besides, he
became interested in what was going on
around him, and it diverted his mind, for a
few brief moments, to watch it. Presently,
the heavy baize curtain, that screened one
of the confessionals, parted, and a woman
issued thence. She had evidently been
weeping, for she was wiping her eyes as
she came out, but her face was illumined
with joy. She entered the body of the
church and took a seat just in front of
Hindes. As she knelt down to return
thanks for her absolution, he ever heard
her murmur, 'Oh! the comfort! the comfort! Thank God for it!' He watched
her earnestly after that, saw her take out
her rosary, and begin to tell her beads,
with her eyes raised and the same look of
happiness irradiating her features. He
found himself wondering what she had

had to confess, and if it was anything like
—like—what he might have to say.   She
looked a good, kindly sort of woman, and
when, after a few minutes spent in prayer,
she rose and left the church, Henry Hindes
rose also and followed her into the open
street.   She looked astonished when she
saw him hurrying after her—still more so
when he began to speak.   She thought at
first she must have dropped something
in her seat, but her little hand-bag and
umbrella were safe.   What could this
stranger want with her?   Her surprise
was still greater when he opened his lips.

'Forgive me for addressing you,' he
commenced, 'but do tell me, is confession such a marvellous consolation to
you?'

The woman looked as if she thought he
wished to insult her.

'Sir,' she replied, 'I saw you in church
just now.   Surely you can answer that
question from your own experience?'

'I cannot.   I was in the church, it is
true, but I am not of your faith.   But you

looked so happy, so grateful, as you left the
confessional, that you almost made me wish
I were. Do tell me. Does confession
really relieve your mind? Does it make
your sins fall off you like an old garment?
My friends have told me so, but I cannot
believe it.'

'Oh, sir, your friends were right, indeed. It is the greatest comfort anyone
can have. Why, when the priest absolves
you, they are all gone. You not only
need not trouble yourself about them
again, but you are strictly forbidden to
do so. It would be doubting God's goodness, and the power He has imparted to
His priests. Oh, sir, do try it, only just
once,' continued the woman, who saw in
Hindes a possible convert. 'Just go to
dear Father Henniker on the right hand
side of the church, and he will explain it
all to you so much better than I can.'

'But will this father, as you call him,
see my face?'

'Oh, no; he sits behind a grating and
you seem to be quite alone with God.

You must put your mouth close to the grating and whisper low, but he will hear every word you say. And then the happiness of absolution! You wont know yourself afterwards. I feel to-day as if I could dance and sing.'

'Thank you, thank you, but I only asked for curiosity. You are very good to have told me so much. Good-afternoon!'

And, raising his hat to her, Hindes went on his way. He had not meant to take advantage of what he had heard, but somehow, whenever he went out, his feet seemed drawn to the same little church, until it became quite a habit of his to go and sit there and watch the penitents. And one day, almost before he knew what he was doing, he had lifted the baize curtain of one of the confessionals and walked inside.

CHAPTER V.

FREDERICK Walcheren had passed through his novitiate, and been ordained. The die was cast. He was a priest. At first his duties were much the same as they had been during his stay in college, with the exception of ministering at the Mass. But, as he settled down into his new position, they became more various. The church to which he was attached was a very small one, belonging to his own sect of the Servite fathers. It had only two priests attached to it, one of whom was presently bound on a mission to the East. When he left, Frederick Walcheren (or Father Walcheren as we must henceforward term him) was to take his place. The novice entered on his new sphere of action, dully, almost sullenly. He knew

he was unfit for the office he had under-
taken, and was mad with himself for not
having had more moral courage than to
accept it, and more moral fortitude to brave
the sneers, or the reproaches which would
have accompanied his relinquishment of
the sacred office he had once believed
himself able and willing to fill. As he
glanced round at his companions during
their hours of privacy, and read the in-
difference on one face, the weariness on
another, the melancholy on a third, and
listened to the stilted speech they considered it a sign of their calling to adopt,
he felt like the startled novice in Gustave
Dore's famous picture, who has his eyes
opened all at once to the earthliness of
his surroundings—to the truth that, Church
or no Church, man's nature is the same,
and God can subdue it just as well whilst
he remains in the world, perhaps better,
than when he has given up the outward
and visible sign of participation in it.

One of Frederick's first duties, naturally,
lay amongst the poor of his parish, and, in

this department, he received a severe re-
buke before long, from his superior, Father
Henniker, for not adopting a more distinctly clerical form of speech when speaking with them of their various ailments
and troubles. In this dilemma, Frederick
had recourse to the counsel of his other
priestly companion, Father Grogan.

Dennis Grogan was an Irishman, a man
several years younger than Frederick Walcheren, but who had entered the ministry
some time before. He was a genial, good-
hearted young fellow, though somewhat
unrefined, as Irish priests are apt to be, and
Walcheren felt less difficulty in talking to
him than to his superior.

' Brother Grogan,' he said one day when
they found themselves, for a few rare
minutes, alone and at liberty, ' how did
you feel when you first became a priest?
Was it not all very strange to you ? '

' Strange !' echoed Grogan, without raising his eyes from his missal, ' how could
that be, when my thoughts had been fixed
on nothing else for years beforehand ? '

'But it is so difficult all at once to shake off the habits and customs of the world. For instance, I have been used all my life to plunge into a bath as soon as I get out of bed, but Brother Henniker has given me a long string of reasons, with none of which I agree, why it is desirable that I should relinquish the habit.'

'If he thinks so, you are bound to obey him! Why give another thought to such a trifle?'

'A trifle!' cried Frederick, indignantly, 'do you call cleanliness a trifle? Why, it has been part of my religion! When I lost my wife—when I had to give up all that made life endurable to me, I said there was only one thing that might not go after it, and that was cold water! And what harm can there be in it? I feel unfit for anything if I am not clean.'

'Perhaps the undue longing you have for this particular form of luxury is the very reason you are now called upon to give it up, brother,' replied Grogan. 'Remember! there have been men so holy as to give up washing altogether, for the love of God.'

'Dirty beasts!' cried Frederick, involuntarily, and then recalled to the indiscretion of which he had been guilty, by the horror depicted in his companion's eyes, he added, 'But you don't really suppose that we can please the Almighty by not washing our flesh, do you?'

'I know that we cannot please Him, unless we pay the strictest obedience to the commands of our superiors. You have not forgotten the vows you have taken so lately already, surely, Brother Walcheren!'

'Of course not, but I confess I was not prepared to find they included the surveillance of my toilet. However, it will be all one a hundred year hence. When I lost my wife, I lost everything!'

'Brother,' said Grogan, with his eyes still fixed on his book, 'would it not be wiser to leave off alluding to the time when you wallowed in earthly sin? It seems to me that you think of it too much. You have but one bride now, the holy Church,

and you owe all your thoughts and affections and aspirations to her.'

'Do you mean that it is sin to think of,
or allude to, my dear lost angel?' demanded
Frederick.

'I think our superior would say that
it is your bounden duty to put all the
memories of the time when you lived with
sinful companions, in a sinful condition, on
one side.'

'Sinful companions!' exclaimed Frederick, all the old man springing up in him
at once. 'Do you mean to tell me you are
alluding to my late wife?'

'I was certainly alluding to the time of
sin, which, by God's grace, we trust you
have put away from you for ever.'

'*Sinful!*' repeated Frederick, with a
glowing face; 'why, she was as fresh and
innocent as the dawn. She was worth all
the priests that were ever ordained put
together! Sinful! It is all very well for
you and me to talk about our sins, acted
and unacted, but never couple her memory
in my presence again with such a word,

Brother Grogan, or I will not answer for myself!'

And the newly-ordained priest rushed from the apartment to subdue his unholy temper in the privacy of his own dormitory.

The conversation was duly reported to Father Henniker, who made a note of it, with the intention of shipping Brother Walcheren to some convenient station, a good distance from London, as soon as possible. He was a brand plucked from the burning, but the brand was smoking considerably still. The fire was not yet quenched, and required a good deal more cold water poured on it before it should be. So he sent Frederick much oftener amongst the poor. Here it was most palpably borne in upon him that he had mistaken his mission. He found no difficulty in talking to his poorer brethren, for he had a kind and generous heart, and he felt deeply for their privations and sufferings. But he found he was too apt to talk with them over their troubles, and advise them on the best way to get out of

them, instead of praying with them and
exhorting them to bless the Hand that
had afflicted them. He detected himself
more than once lamenting that he had no
private purse from which he could have
relieved their poverty, and telling them
not to rise when he entered the room, and
pay him so much well-meant attention
when they were not fit to leave their seats.
Once or twice he gave vent to an expression, or a wish, that shocked himself—
pulled him up short, as it were, as he had
been used to pull up his horses, in the
olden days, upon their haunches, in order
to check their too animated career. But,
for a priest! Frederick's constant inward
cry now was, 'Why did I ever suppose I
was fit to become a priest?'

The face and form of his wife seemed to
haunt him as much as they did Henry
Hindes, and he could not bring himself to
confess, to his fellow-priests, how constantly
he thought and dreamed of her! He
knew he should do so—he had been reared
in the belief that, if he omitted one sin in

confession, the whole was null and void,
and absolution a mockery. Yet, he could
not, and he would not, mention Jenny's
name. He consoled himself with the idea
that it was not a sin ; that she was an
angel in heaven, and he might dream of
her just as soon as of the Virgin Mary, or
any other saint. Still, the fact remained
that, where he had sworn to render im-
plicit obedience, he was thinking and act-
ing for himself, just as if he still inhabited
that world which he had voluntarily given
up.

This tale is not written with the view of
defending him. It only endeavours to
portray the workings of a mind that has
promised to give itself up into another
man's keeping, and finds that it cannot do
so without resigning its liberty of conscience—its rights as a man and a child of
God—all its strength, its decision and its
humanity.

Frederick Walcheren had not yet been
made a confessor. He was considered to
be too much of a novice—too young, and,

perhaps, too handsome for so difficult an
office.   And, in truth, he did not desire it.
He had received instruction in the duties
of the confessional, and they did not attract
him.   He said openly that he feared he
should never gain the *sangfroid* necessary
for such a delicate duty.   He had been a
man of the world, accustomed to restrain
his language and his allusions before
women, and the questions he was advised
to put to young girls, both of the educated
and uneducated classes, shocked him to the
last degree.   He felt that he never could
ask them, never mind how long he might
be at the work—that he should feel himself
blushing all over, just as if he were in a
drawing-room instead of a confessional.
He confided these scruples to his director,
who begged him not to worry himself on
the subject—that it would all come natural
to him in time, and that, if his scruples did
not vanish with custom, there were plenty
of other fields open to him beside the confessional.

The little church which he belonged to

was called Saint Sebastian del Torriano.
Confessions were heard there on every day
of the week, if necessary, but the regular
time for them was on Saturdays, between
three and six in the afternoon, when Fathers
Henniker and Grogan were always ready
to receive their penitents, whilst Frederick
conducted Benediction. On one particular
Saturday, however, just as the clock was
on the stroke of three, Father Grogan
came hurriedly into the priests' house, to
tell Frederick that Father Henniker had
been taken very ill with spasms of the
heart, and was totally unable to hear confessions. *He* was therefore to occupy the
confessional instead of him, and they had
sent round to another church to ask the
services of a brother priest for Benediction,
which did not commence until four o'clock.
Frederick was rather taken aback by this
intelligence; however, there was nothing
to be done but to cast aside his book, don
his priestly vestment, and ensconce himself
in Father Henniker's confessional.

There were only two confessionals in

Saint Sebastian del Torriano, one on each side of the chancel. They were divided into two parts, the closed box where the priest sat, and the open portion, which was shaded by red baize curtains, where the penitent knelt. Between these was a partition formed of perforated zinc. This rendered everything behind it dark to the penitent. All he or she saw was the sheet of zinc, through which their sins or troubles had to be whispered in the confessor's ear. The priest, on the contrary, could see the features and expressions of the penitents plainly, on account of the light thrown behind them by the opening of the curtains, which were too narrow to draw quite close. Few of the penitents knew this. It gave them confidence to believe they were unseen or recognised, and only the *habitués* of the church cared to discover their identity. Father Walcheren walked into the confessional, feeling rather sheepish, and a little shy. He soon found, however, that the penitents left him but little to do. They provided all the talk themselves, and

came laden with a string of small vices to
pour at his feet, with perfect confidence
of hearing the mechanical absolution pronounced over them as soon as the list was
completed. They were, for the most part,
women, both young and old. Some were
in a tremendous hurry. He could watch
them from the body of the church fighting
their way into the confessional to get their
business over as quickly as possible, almost
pushing their neighbours aside in order to
reach him first. They were accustomed to
confess regularly every Saturday afternoon,
and did it as formally as they assumed
their walking things to go out. But they
were in a bit of a hurry. They were going
on to Mrs So-and-So's afternoon tea, or a
flower *fête* at the Botanical, or, perhaps,
down to the Crystal Palace to see a dog
or cat show afterwards, and had promised
not to keep mamma waiting. Others,
again, were old women, who brought not
only their own sins, but those of all their
household, into the confessional with them
—related how bad their servants were, and

what difficulty they experienced in keeping their husbands in the straight and narrow path. This sort of penitent showed no disposition whatever to hasten, was deaf, indeed, to all the coughs that went on outside to remind them that time was up, nor took any notice of the faces that occasionally peered round the curtain to see if the confessor and confessed had both fallen asleep, or died at their posts.

Frederick Walcheren felt sick and disgusted with his fellow-creatures as he sat in Father Henniker's place and listened to the mechanical details of their faults and follies. Not one had approached him in a sincere manner or an earnest voice. It had all been rattle, rattle, prattle, prattle, get-it-over-as-quick-as-you-can sort of work, without any evidences of faith, or feeling, or hearty repentance for the sins they had committed. They had been told it was a religious duty—they knew they couldn't go to Holy Communion the next morning unless they had confessed—and had they gone to bed that night without having done so, they would have felt quite uneasy, because it had been their custom for years, and not because they had any real penitence in their hearts. Frederick Walcheren was musing much after this fashion, and pronouncing the absolution upon one after another, wondering when the long string would have come to an end, when the curtain was raised again and a man stumbled into the confessional. He did not ask a blessing, but, as old Catholics seldom do, knowing that as soon as they sink on their knees it will be given them, Frederick pronounced it in the usual form, and waited for the confession to follow. To his intense surprise, the first words the man said were,—

'I am not of your faith.'

His voice was so weak and husky that Frederick Walcheren did not at first recognise it.

'Indeed!' he answered, in a low whisper. 'Then why are you here?'

'Because I have a burden on my soul, an intolerable burden, and I am told that, if I

confess it, it will leave me. Will you give
me absolution ?'

Frederick now looked at the stranger
more particularly. He thought he had
heard his voice before, and, now he saw him
plainly, he recognised, to his intense astonishment, Henry Hindes. Yes! decidedly
Henry Hindes—the man for whom he had
always had such an invincible dislike, without knowing why—but so changed, in the
short space of a year, that he thought he
should never have known him again had he
not heard him speak. His first impulse was
to reveal his identity ; the next moment he
remembered where he was, and for what purpose, and shrunk further back on his seat, as
if it were possible that the penitent should
see him as plainly as he was seen. But, when
he addressed him again, he was careful to
disguise his own voice, and to speak as low
as possible.

'I cannot say if I can give you absolution,' he answered, 'until I have heard your
confession. But God never refuses it to
the truly penitent.'

'I *am* penitent, God knows!' replied Hindes. 'My life is a misery to me on account of my sin. I would wash it out with my life's blood if it were possible.'

'I am listening to you,' was all the answer that the priest made.

'Are you quite, *quite* sure that no one will hear me?' demanded the unhappy man.

'No one but the God you have offended and myself,' said Frederick, in the same assumed tone; 'but place your mouth close to the grating, and speak low.'

Hindes did as was required of him, and began,—

'I have committed a murder! Is there any hope for me?'

'A murder!' exclaimed the priest, startled; and then, remembering himself, he added, 'there is hope for all!'

'It was a girl,' resumed Hindes, in a shaking voice; 'I had known her from her childhood, and I had secretly loved her. She taunted me whilst we were standing near some cliffs, and in my rage I— God forgive me!—I pushed her over them.'

Frederick Walcheren was nearly rushing out of the confessional and seizing his penitent by the throat; but he restrained himself in time. But he could not, speak plainly. He sat in his box, paralysed with horror and his desire for revenge. How could he fail to guess what was coming! The murderer of his Jenny knelt before him. He knew it for a certainty, but he forced himself to reply,—

'Go on! Tell all!'

'I loved her,' wailed Henry Hindes; 'I would have given my life for hers at any time, but she preferred another man, and ran away and married him. I was commissioned by her father to pursue them and bring her back, if possible. I followed her to Dover, and met her on the cliffs. She was so lovely, so haughty in her pride and love for that other man, that she drove me mad. I reasoned with her. She said she hated me—had always done so— should do so to the end. It was her defiant words that raised the devil in me I saw her standing perilously near the edge

of the cliffs as she spoke to me, and put
out my hand to prevent an accident.   I
grasped her by the wrist.   She thought I
was going to lay violent hands on her,
and calling out, " Don't touch me !   Do
you want to murder me ?" wrenched her
hand from mine.   She put it into my head.
I swear before God I never thought of
it before.   But, when she said those words,
the idea of preventing anybody ever having
her, since *I* could not, flashed into my
brain, and I pushed her—God forgive me !
I put out my hand and pushed her over
the cliff.   That is the whole truth ; but
I have been a miserable man ever since,
and Heaven has avenged itself upon me !
My only son has fallen down a flight of
stairs, and is likely to be a cripple for
life.   Give me absolution !   I am truly
penitent !   Lift this awful burden off my
soul, and let me feel I am forgiven.'

The priest did not answer, but sat in
his box, with set teeth and clenched hands,
thinking, if he had his will, what he would
do to the wretch who had robbed him, in

so brutal a manner, of his beautiful young wife.

'Speak to me! I implore you,' wailed Henry Hindes. 'I thought this confession would ease my soul, but it feels no better. I repeat I am truly penitent! Why cannot I have absolution? Is it because I am not of your faith? I will promise to become a Catholic to - morrow if that will bring me any peace. Speak! pray, speak!'

At last Frederick Walcheren understood that he must say something, or his conduct would be open to misconstruction, but his voice sounded like that of an old man; no need to disguise it now.

'Absolution,' he replied, 'is for the truly penitent. There, you are right! But the truly penitent make amends, for the wrongs they have committed, to the world as well as to God. A foul, uncalled-for murder needs expiation according to the law, as well as before heaven. The blood of your victim cries to you from the ground. I have no power to pronounce

absolution over you until you have made
what reparation the law demands.'

'Do you mean that I must confess it
before men?' asked Hindes, in a cold
sweat with terror.

'Most certainly! You owe it to all of
whom you stole her life! You think only
of your own misery and fear! What of her
husband's—her parents'—the society which
delighted in her youth, and beauty, and
innocence? Make your peace with them
first, and then ask forgiveness of God.'

'Oh! I cannot, I cannot! I am a
married man myself. I have a wife and
children dependent on me! God cannot
wish me to own this deed—this accident—
it was more an accident than anything else.
I did not think what I was doing. My
rage—my desire of revenge overcame my
better feelings. Had I stopped to consider for a moment, I should never have
done it. But there was no time. It
happened so suddenly, before I realised
what my hasty touch would do. Oh! father,
surely it will not be accounted against me

as a murder. I was wrong to call it by such a
name. It was an accident! a pure accident!'

The priest's voice came back like a
judgment.

'I do not believe you, Henry Hindes.'

'You know my name,' cried the penitent, starting. 'Who are you?'

'One whom you also know, or have
known, but that is irrelevant to the matter
in hand.'

'You are mistaken! I know no priest,
nor have ever known one,' replied Hindes,
trembling.

All his anxiety now was to get out of
the confessional before the priest, who
had evidently recognised his voice, should
also see his face. He little knew that
he had been gazing at it all the while,
noting its expression, and watching every
change that passed over it.

'You are quite mistaken,' he continued
hurriedly; 'I am not the person you mentioned, nor have I ever heard the name
before. I am a tradesman from the North
of England, and am only passing through

town. I hoped to hear better news from you, but it is of no consequence. I cannot stay any longer. Good-afternoon !'

And then, his cunning coming to his aid, he added,—

'I have been only trying to see how far I could go with you. A friend told me I could get absolution for every sin in the calendar, so I thought I would make up a story about a murder. I suppose it was very wrong of me, but we had a bet on the subject, and I wanted to prove to him that I was right. I trust you will forgive me.'

As he said the last words, he left the confessional, and prepared to fly from the church. But, as he did so, the door which admitted the confessor to his portion of the confessional also opened, and the face of Frederick Walcheren looked forth from it. Hindes turned involuntarily, and met his gaze, and with a low cry turned round and literally ran out of the sacred building.

CHAPTER VI.

HE had known so little of Frederick Walcheren before Jenny's death, and he had so
purposely avoided thrusting himself in his
way afterwards, that he had not had the
slightest intimation that he had entered the
Catholic Church as a priest. The dis-
covery was as great a shock to him as his
revelation had been to his auditor. How
he ever got back to Hampstead on that
eventful afternoon, he never knew. His
head and heart were in as rapid a whirl as
they had been when he committed the
murder; the murder which, he now made
sure, would, sooner or later, land him on the
gallows. There was but one chance for
him—the alleged secrecy of the confessional. Could he trust to it? Would Fred-

erick Walcheren's vows prove adamant against the awful news he had been called upon to hear—the strong desire to avenge his wife's death which must be raging in his breast at the present moment, unless, on assuming his priestly robes, he had parted with his manhood. Henry Hindes pondered over this question, night and day, for a wonder, morphia-free.

The shock of discovering *who* was his confessor had acted on him as it might have done on a drunkard. It had sobered him, and, for a while, he conceived a horror of the drug without which he had considered it impossible he could live. Instinct came to his assistance, and made him feel he must keep his wits about him, in readiness for what might happen. After all, no one had, or could ever have, any proof against him. And who would believe the word of a priest from evidence taken in the confessional? What witness was there to what he had confessed? Besides, had he not cancelled it all at the last, by saying it had been the outcome of a bet between himself and a friend, and why should he not stick to that story?

Still, the knowledge that he had shared his secret with any living being rankled in his mind, and, after some days' cogitation with himself, he made up his mind to seek out Walcheren and ascertain what he intended to do in the matter.   If his position as confessor prohibited him from taking any steps to disclose what had been confided to him, things would remain as they were before; if, on the contrary, he should betray the least disposition to bring him to justice, he would fly the country at once and leave no trace behind him.

Meanwhile, he had left Frederick in a state of mind hardly more enviable.   He was unable to quit the confessional directly the murderer of his wife disappeared. Several people were waiting to push their way into his presence, directly he was at liberty.   So he was compelled to sit there, whilst they poured their plaints into his deaf ears, and he pronounced the absolution over sins of which he had taken no

heed. Who can blame him? He was a
priest, it is true, but he was a man still, a
lover, and a widower. Hindes' hateful
confession had revived all the holiest, the
tenderest, the most passionately-mourned
portion of his existence. He was no longer
in the confessional. He was with his beloved and murdered Jenny, in the Castle
Warden at Dover—in the ballrooms of
Hampstead—out on the breezy heath, or
in her pretty phaeton. She was with her
lover and her husband once more, not as
an angel from Heaven, or a pale corpse
lying in her cambric shroud, but as Jenny
—his laughing, saucy, living, lovely Jenny,
in whom he had taken such rapturous de-
light, and of whom this man—this fiend—
this devil—had robbed him in the basest
and most cruel manner. He could think
of nothing else. His heart throbbed as
though he should suffocate. He longed
to rush out into the open air, but he was
condemned to keep his place until Benediction was concluded and the confessions
were over. Then he went straight to the

sacristy and disrobed. He could not go through the mockery of a prayer. Rage was causing his whole frame to tremble. Curses, not blessings, were on his lips. He would not insult his Maker by addressing Him whilst in so earthly a mood. Father Grogan, who usually remained on his knees for about an hour after service, heaved a sigh as he saw the newly-ordained priest tear out of the church as if he had had more than enough of it, and put up an extra petition, good soul, for his impatient and undisciplined companion.

But Frederick Walcheren knew nothing of it. He was hastening with all dispatch, and in a state of the greatest excitement, to seek an interview with his superior. But Father Henniker was unable to see him. The heart spasms, which he occasionally suffered from, had been more violent than usual, and the doctor had ordered him to see no one that evening. So Father Walcheren sent up an entreaty for leave of absence on business of an important nature, which was immediately granted him. He was bursting with the intelligence which had been communicated to him. He felt that he must consult some friend as to the action he should take concerning it. He could not wait until the morning. It was coming between him and all his duties. Since he could not see Father Henniker, he would ask for an interview with his old friend, Father Tasker. So it was at his residence that he presented himself, late in the evening.

'What is the matter, my dear brother?' demanded Father Tasker. 'You look agitated.'

'Agitated!' echoed Frederick, 'I am bewildered—mad!'

'Why, whatever can be the reason? You alarm me by such violent expressions.'

'Father Tasker, you have known my story from the beginning—all my fears, hopes, misery and despair. You know how my beloved wife was snatched from me; how I mourned her loss, and wondered over the mystery of it.'

'Yes, yes; but forgive me, my dear

friend, I hoped these sad thoughts had all been swallowed up in the love of God and the blessings of His holy Church.'

'They will never be swallowed up by anything so long as my life lasts,' cried Frederick, in his old impetuous way, 'but while I believed God had taken her from me, I could be, in a measure, resigned to His will.   But to-day I have found out that it was *not* by His will that we were so cruelly separated.   She was murdered! Killed by a man! Pushed over those cruel cliffs!—oh! my poor darling, why did I let you leave my sight for one moment? Why was I not there to protect you from his villainy?—and dashed to pieces on the beach beneath, out of a spirit of wicked jealousy and revenge!   And I have come to ask you to tell me, as a man, *what shall I do?*   Think of the days when you were free, when you, too, perhaps, loved and lost, and advise me how to act, to bring this murderer to justice?'

Father Tasker was visibly affected by this recital.   He had not yet forgotten what it was to feel like a man, and the distress of poor Frederick Walcheren touched him to the quick.

'My poor lad,' he replied, forgetting for the moment the sacred office which his young friend had taken upon himself, 'I am deeply grieved to hear this story. I had so hoped that your new and blessed duties would completely drive all such memories from your mind. To have them renewed in this painful manner is most distressing. But where did you hear this intelligence, Frederick? Are you sure that it is correct, or only a base rumour set up to annoy you?'

'I heard it in the confessional,' replied the young priest.

'In the confessional?'

'Yes; Father Henniker was taken suddenly ill this afternoon, with one of his heart attacks, and I was called upon to take his place. After a while a man entered, whom I recognised at the first glance. It was—'

'Hush! hush! stop my dear brother;

what are you thinking of?' exclaimed the
elder priest, warningly. 'You must not
repeat any names. Remember, the confessional is sacred.'

'All right, father, I won't ; but it will
have to come out some day. Well, this
man entered, and after telling me he was
not a Catholic, said he had a great burthen
on his mind and wished to try if confession
would ease it. He then went on to give
me the whole details of my darling's
murder—how he had gone down to Dover
and met her on the cliffs, and she had
repulsed and taunted him—I can see her
doing it, my poor, brave girl!—and how
he had pushed her deliberately over the
rocks to the shingles below. He said he
had been miserable ever since, as well
he may have been, the brute! and had the
audacity to ask me for absolution for his
crime.'

'Did you give it him ?'

'Not I! I felt much more like giving
him his quietus for evermore ! I told him,
if he were penitent, to go and make his

peace with the law first, and then ask for
the forgiveness of Heaven. It was all I
could do to speak to him with any degree
of decency.'

'Do you think he did not recognise you,
brother?'

'Not till the last, when I opened the
half door and looked at him. He knew
me then and ran away, horrified, no doubt,
at his own indiscretion. And now, father,
tell me what steps can I take? To whom
should I go? I feel as if I could not pass
through the Sunday services with this black
secret in my keeping. Tell me downright,
what shall I do?'

Father Tasker looked at him sadly.

'You should know better than to ask
me. You can do nothing!'

'*Nothing?* Are you laughing at my
agony?'

'God forbid! I am grieving for this
fresh pain you are called upon to endure,
more than I can say. But I repeat, you
can do nothing. Have you forgotten the
solemn vows you have taken not to reveal

anything you may hear in the confessional ?
You would not have dreamt of coming to me
with a story you might have heard concerning a stranger. Your hands are just as much
tied when the revelation affects yourself!'

'You mean that I can do nothing to set
this matter right—that I am bound to let
the murderer of my wife go free?'

'Certainly, since he has confessed the
deed to you in your sacred office as confessor! You are bound by your own oath
to maintain an utter silence on the subject.'

'And he, this brute, is to walk about
the world, prosperous and esteemed—
triumphing, perhaps, in his secret crimes
—whilst my innocent darling lies unavenged in her grave? Oh! it is too, *too*
cruel! I cannot believe it would be a
duty!'

'It is a duty, a duty which you could
only overcome by breaking your most
solemn word, by violating your sanctity as
a priest, by disgracing your holy office and
bringing discredit on the sacrament of
confession. What are you thinking of

Frederick? What would you have thought in the olden days if *I*, for example, had revealed to the world what you have told me in the confessional?'

'Oh, that was different,' exclaimed the young priest passionately. 'My confessions —most people's confessions—are of trivial, everyday faults. But this—this heinous murder, which cries aloud to God's Throne for vengeance—is not the same thing. If murderers and such like criminals are to believe that, by coming to us and depositing their vile secrets in the confessional, they may obtain relief and absolution, the Church will be turned into a depository for crime—a sink hole of wickedness without any judgment to follow.'

'Whatever you may think, Frederick, the fact remains that, as a priest, you cannot reveal this terrible secret, nor even breathe a hint that you have heard it. With me you are safe, but to no one else must you mention the subject. Go home, my dear brother, and pray to forget it, even to forgive it.'

'*Never!*' cried the young man, emphatically. 'I should lie if I said I should ever do either one or the other. Father Tasker, I have had many doubts, as you know, since entering the Church, whether I have not made a grave mistake, but I have none at the present moment. I see that I have put myself in a wrong position. Had I had the least idea of what I have heard to-day—had I imagined, however vaguely, that my precious wife had come unfairly by the death which I always believed to be due to an accident, nothing would have induced me to bind myself by any vows but those which should bring her murderer to justice. And now that the bitter truth has been accidentally revealed to me—that I have met the villain face to face—you tell me I must be silent, that I must brood over my deep wrongs for a lifetime, praying the while, perhaps, for the welfare of the brute who goes scot-free. But I cannot do it—I cannot! I wear the vestments of a priest, but I am a man all the same, a man who loves and has lost,

who knows his enemy and thirsts for
revenge! And you bid me have patience
and keep silence. It is impossible! unnatural! You lay a task on me that I am
unable to fulfil.'

'You shock me,' said the old priest.
'You are indeed right, with such feelings,
to say you should never have accepted the
office you fill. What are you saying?
You cannot, and you will not, and it is
unnatural that you should. You forget
you are no longer a free agent, but must
do as the Church commands you—not as
you think, or feel.'

The Church may unfrock me, but she
cannot unmake me a man, with all a man's
feelings and desires. My love I buried in
the grave with my darling, cheerfully, for
the Church's sake. All my earthly amusements and luxuries I have been willing to
give up in the same way. Life has nothing much left in it for me now, and I am
desirous to dedicate the rest of it, if needful, to the good of my brethren. But this
is something quite different. This is a

duty, in my own estimation—the blood of
my dearest possession crying out to me for
vengeance from the ground.   I say, her
murderer shall not live to murder other
victims, perhaps in the same cold-blooded,
heartless manner!   God's justice and the
world's laws demand it.   It would be a
sacrilege to let him go free!'

'And I repeat, Frederick, that if the
man had confessed to slaying the Christ
Himself, in the confessional, you could not,
as a priest, have betrayed him.   If he
comes to you again, you can counsel him
to make the only reparation in his power,
by confessing his sin to the world, and
bearing the penalty, but you can go no
further.'

'As if a mean-spirited cur like that, who
would stoop to wage war against a helpless
girl, would be brave enough to swing for
it!' cried Frederick, contemptuously. 'Not
he!   When I told him I knew his name,
he tried to get out of what he had said, by
pretending he had confessed a made-up
story for a bet, but, when he saw my face,

his told a different tale. What man, born
of woman, could remain dumb under such
circumstances? It shames his manhood to
think of it. There is not a creature in this
vast city that, knowing what I know, would
not deliver the criminal up to justice.'

'Perhaps so. To conceal a crime under
ordinary circumstances is to be a partner
in its guilt. Had this wretched man told
you of his sin anywhere else than where
he did—had you been with him in the open
street, or in your private rooms, you would
be justified in refusing to keep his secret
for him, even though you are a priest. But
he came to you, believing that he was safe
in speaking openly to a confessor; therefore, to betray his confidence would be to
perjure yourself, and without effecting your
object. You could not take the secrets of
the confessional into an open court of law
as witness of a man's guilt. Who would
accept your testimony? How easy it
would be for the murderer to turn round,
as you say he attempted to do, and deny
that it was anything but a jest. Where

would you be then ?   Disgraced, but unavenged.'

'You are right, father,' said Frederick,
with a deep sigh, as he rose to leave, 'and
I have been an impetuous idiot.   Thanks
for all your kindness and patience with me.
I fear I try it sorely at times.   Good-night!'

He went back to his residence, but the
father's last words rung in his ears meanwhile.   'Had this man told you of his
guilt anywhere else.'   Would it be possible
to induce Hindes to repeat what he had
said in the confessional elsewhere ?   Would
he be too astute, too cunning, too incredul-
ous of the safety of such a thing, to repeat
his story ?   Or might he, if Frederick
could only conceal his hatred of him sufficiently well, be cajoled into believing that
'once a priest was always a priest,' and
that the oath of silence was as obligatory
out of the confessional as in ?   The young
man shuddered as he thought of encounter-
ing Hindes again, yet, for Jenny's sake—
Jenny, who had said, 'poor child, almost
prophetically, how she hated and mistrusted

this man—he could manage, he thought, to hide his aversion and loathing, if it would serve the purpose of causing him to betray himself, with confidence, under conditions when he could take advantage of it to deliver him over to justice.

'Oh, what feelings are these?' cried Frederick, in his inmost soul. 'Why did I ever become a priest? I had much better have enlisted in the army. I am not fitted for my position. I told them all so, but they would drive me into it. How can I go on offering the Mass, and attending all the services of the Church, with these burning desires for revenge in my heart? In another fashion I am as bad as this brute Hindes. He goes about the world as a whited sepulchre, and so do I. I wonder if I shall ever have the courage to break off my fetters. It would be one bold stroke and I should be free again. People would say, "How shocking. Fancy, he was a Catholic priest!" and poor dear Father Tasker and my cousin Philip would declare I was lost for evermore; but would their saying so, or thinking so, make it a fact? Which is better, that I should give up an office for which I am not only unfit, but in which I am a living lie, or go on with it, dissatisfied with myself and all my surroundings? After all, God, who knows my thoughts and my intentions, is the only Person Whose opinion I should fear, and I know that He hates hypocrisy. One thing I am sure of, that I cannot live a life of inactivity whilst my angel's death is unavenged, and her murderer goes at large. The prayers would blister my tongue. I am unfit for any of my sacred duties whilst such thoughts fill my mind. I wish—I wish, from my inmost soul, that I was a better man, but I am very earthly yet. Every thought proves it. And yet, oh, my God! I shall not serve Thee worse in the world than here. Thou knowest, Who knowest all things, that I shall not return to the world I left. That has fled with all its pleasures, but this life cramps me. I am not myself. I have made a mistake. Show me how to remedy it.'

These were the thoughts that occupied
the mind of Frederick Walcheren, and he
was not a hypocrite in giving vent to
them. He had been a very wild and self-
seeking man before he knew Jenny Crampton, thinking only of the gratification of his
senses, and caring nothing for the things
of the other world. But the Catholic
Church makes religion so much more
realistic than any other. She depicts the
saints and angels as being so much nearer
to us in an earthly sense—walking by our
sides as we journey through life, and taking an interest in all our troubles and
pleasures (as, indeed, all the souls departed do), that her votaries, especially
those who have been reared in her faith,
find it most difficult to shake off her influence, or to forget her precepts. It is said
that a Protestant may be converted to
Catholicism, or Mahommedanism, or Spirit-
ualism, or any other 'ism'; but a Catholic,
if he once rejects the faith of his fathers,
becomes nothing but a total disbeliever.
He either believes all or nothing. This

may or may not be true, but the exception
proves the rule. At all events, though his
wife's death had not fitted Frederick Walcheren to be a priest, it had made him think
very deeply, and the lessons he had learned
in his youth had returned with twofold
force upon his mind, and made him view
his past life in a light which would prevent
his ever returning to it. He viewed his
past career now as it really had been—the
outcome of his selfish desires — and he
mourned over its effects sincerely.

Amongst his other sins, the one he had
committed against Rhoda Berry haunted
him. The other women he had trifled
with had either been very well able to
take care of themselves, or they had been
more sinning than sinned against. Rhoda
Berry, of them all, had used only the
weapon of her own love against him, had
suffered the most in consequence, and had
complained the least. It was strange that
he—a priest—should find his thoughts
turning most to her—a simple, uneducated
girl—in this dilemma. But he saw plainly

that he must expect no help from his fellow-clergy. They had relinquished the world, with all things pertaining thereto, and would only advise him to pray and be patient, and regard his present state of miserable uncertainty as a trial sent from Heaven out of loving-kindness, and his thirsting to avenge the cruel murder of his wife as a sore temptation from the Enemy of Mankind, which it was his solemn duty to trample under foot. And then this inability to disclose anything heard under the seal of confession! If that were true, Frederick felt he could not lend himself to be the depositary of state secrets, the keeping of which might be, perhaps, a wrong to his sovereign, his country and the people at large.

So he sat down and wrote a note to Rhoda Berry, in which he called her his dear friend, and said that, if she were likely to be visiting London again, he would much like to see her for a few minutes and receive her in the common parlour of the priests' house, or call upon her at any place she might prefer. Rhoda showed this letter to her mother, and her mother, as usual, went to the cards for advice. The oracle said, decidedly, ' Yes.' Rhoda was to visit town for the express purpose of seeing her late lover, and the journey would be productive of good for both of them.

' I can't say I see what luck can come of it,' said Rhoda. ' If Fred were not yet ordained, I might dissuade him from it, but I said all I could last time we met, and I might as well have talked to the table. I can't fancy him a priest, mother! It seems too ridiculous. I often think what baby will look like some day, when he is grown up and bothers to know who his father is, and I tell him a Catholic priest. He'll think I'm out of my mind.'

' Don't worry over that now, my girl,' replied Mrs Berry, ' there's plenty of time before you. Little Fred won't trouble himself about his father for many years to come. And there's no saying what may happen before that comes to pass! I often fancy things will turn out different from what you imagine. You'll have a happy life after all. I'm sure of that, whoever you may pass it with.'

'It'll never be happy passed away from Fred, mother. You may take your oath of that,' said Rhoda, shaking her head; 'but I'll go up and see him, poor fellow, all the same. I never refused him anything yet, worse luck! and I can't begin now.'

CHAPTER VII.

FREDERICK WALCHEREN did not rest satisfied with the ultimatum which Father Tasker had passed on his conduct, with regard to what he had learned in the confessional. He had no hope of obtaining a different opinion, but he considered it right, before he acted on his own responsibility, to leave no stone unturned to vindicate his idea of what was just and right. As soon as Father Henniker was sufficiently recovered to be able to resume his duties, he sought an audience with him, and told him the whole story, carefully withholding any details that might lead to the identification of the parties concerned.

The older priest was very much shocked by the recital. He felt for his young brother keenly, so he said, but he had no further consolation to give him. It was

a terrible trial for him—sent by Almighty
God to test his faith and endurance of
suffering. It was a high honour conferred
on him by Heaven ; he was called upon to
take up the cross in imitation of the Saviour
of Mankind, and to carry it, maybe, through
life. But there was no remedy except the
medicines which had been already pre-
scribed for him—Prayer and Patience, and
rejoicing in Suffering !

And he was a man with a burning,
aching heart, bowed down beneath a sense
of an irreparable loss, brought on him by
a fellow-man, and he writhed under these
recommendations to inactivity like a strong
man would writhe and chafe to rend apart
the cords that bound him, whilst what he
loved best was being cruelly tortured under
his very eyes.

He did not answer the father for a few
minutes, but sat with his head bowed down
and his eyes fixed upon the ground.

'I fear you do not see this matter in
it's proper light, brother,' said Father
Henniker, after a long pause.

'If yours is the proper light, I cannot!' replied Frederick.

'It is not my light. It is the light of the Church,' said his companion.

'But it has not shined on me,' retorted Frederick, quickly. 'You make me feel I am unfit for our holy office! I am a man still, not a neutral creature, without feelings, or passions, or warm, human blood running through my veins. If I imagined that ordination would cure me of all this, I was mistaken! It has failed to do so. On every side I receive the same advice. Don't feel—don't think—don't remember! Be patient—be calm—be silent! Act, live, do your duty as if such things had never been, as if everything were right within you, and God had not taken the only thing which made your life worth living from you at one cruel blow!'

'Hush! hush!' interposed the priest. 'When you compare the love you conceived for a sinful woman, whose charms only appealed to the lust of the eye, to the duty which you owe to the Almighty, you are uttering blasphemy.'

'A sinful woman!' echoed Frederick. 'Who presumes to call her so? You forget she was my wife, father! No one shall ever call her "sinful" in my hearing, were it the Holy Father himself!'

'I will not listen to such talk any longer,' exclaimed Father Henniker, indignantly. 'You are right when you say you have mistaken your vocation, Brother Walcheren! Leave my presence, and never enter it again whilst such feelings obtain the mastery over you!'

Frederick did as he was desired, biting his lips with indignation at the rebuff, and, retreating to his own room, did not speak to his superior for some days to come.

It was while he was still warring with the human passions which had been raised in his breast, that he was informed one evening that a gentleman desired to speak with him, and on demanding his name, received the card of Henry Hindes. A close observer might have seen Father

Walcheren's hands clench as he read the
name on the card, but he told the man to
admit the visitor to his private sanctum,
in as calm a voice as he could muster.
Whilst Henry Hindes was being conducted
through the long stone passages, Frederick
tried to make up his mind how he should
address him, but his thoughts were all
chaos. He stood like a statue, with his
mind a blank, to receive—the murderer of
his wife.

Hindes entered, looking very cringing
and humiliated. He glanced round the
small, bare chamber on entering, to see if
there was any third person present to listen
to their conversation, but perceiving they
were alone, he plucked up courage to advance a little nearer. He had made up
his mind to learn the worst, for he could
wrestle no longer with his agony of suspense. As he advanced, Frederick Walcheren retreated till the distance of the
room lay between them.

'Not a step nearer, Mr Hindes,' he
ejaculated; 'give me some chance of re-

maining master of myself! Now, what have you to say to me?'

'Are you sure we are quite alone?' inquired his visitor, glancing around him fearfully; 'that we shall not be overheard?'

'No one will hear you,' replied Frederick.

'I know you—you recognised my voice the other day,' commenced Hindes, 'and I felt I must speak to you on the subject. I have understood that every word uttered in the confessional is sacred—that a priest dare not reveal it, even if he would. Is that true?'

'It is true!' replied the other.

'And that a priest's word would not be taken, even if he did repeat what he heard as a confessor—that he would be disgraced and stripped of his cloth in consequence, so that the secrets told in confession are as inviolate as the grave!'

'You have been informed aright. Were it not so, the sacrament of confession would be at a discount. Penitents would be afraid to tell of their sins, the greatest of which

they confide to the ears of their confessor
without the slightest fear.'

' I wanted to make sure I had been informed aright,' continued Hindes, with the
sweat of fear and agitation standing thick
upon his brow, 'so I thought I would
come and ask you straight. You must be
aware that I did not know I was addressing
you last week, Mr Walcheren ; in fact, I
had not heard that you had entered the
Church. Naturally, you would have been
the last person I should have chosen for
such a confidence.'

' Naturally !' repeated Frederick.

' It was an awful thing to have to say,'
said Hindes, trembling ; ' but you assure
me it will go no further. I will do anything to ensure this. Become a Catholic
to-morrow, or leave the country and promise not to return to it. I am truly penitent,
Mr Walcheren, indeed I am, and ready to
prove my sincerity in any way you may
choose to point out to me !'

' I have already told you, sir, that the
secrets of the confessional are inviolate, and

the Church demands no penance except such as shall be pleasing to Almighty God! Since you say you are penitent, you have, doubtless, said the same to Him.'

'Yes, indeed! I have tried to pray, but heaven seems so far off for such as I. But it was hardly a crime. It was more an accident than anything else. If I could only make you believe this.'

'I always did believe it, until your own lips told me otherwise.'

'Yes, yes! but in confession I wished to make the worst of my error, in order to see if I should have absolution for the worst. But it really *was* an accident! I assure you, on my honour.'

'Mr Hindes,' said Father Walcheren, sternly, 'let us have no fooling, if you please! I cannot listen to two stories. Last week you said, distinctly, that you did it by design. Now you want to make out it was an accident. But I shall choose to believe that what you said in the con-fessional, when you thought you were speaking to a stranger, was the true version of the story.'

' It was, it was ; but it is safe with you ! ' cried Hindes, as though he felt himself beaten, and declined to fight any longer. ' I will tell you the whole truth, indeed I will ! It will be a comfort to get it clean off my soul.'

At this critical moment it flashed through Father Walcheren's mind that he should warn his penitent that he was not in the confessional, but he could not. Jenny—his murdered Jenny, seemed to flit before him, with her beautiful features all soiled with the damps of death and almost indistinguishable through corruption, crying aloud for justice on her assassin, and, right or wrong, he could not, and he did not, speak.

' It happened just as I told you the other day,' continued Henry Hindes. ' I loved her—don't be angry with me, it is all over now, you know—and I would not have harmed her for the world, but I loved her long before she ever knew you, and her marriage made me jealous as well as angry. Mr Crampton deputed me to follow her down to Dover and make her an offer to return home, on the condition that she gave you up and allowed her father to annul the marriage, on a plea that you took a false oath concerning her age. When I arrived at the hotel she had gone out, and I wandered on the cliffs to beguile the time, and there I met her.'

'Go on!' said Frederick, curtly.

'I told you the rest,' replied Hindes, beginning to feel uneasy at the other's manner.

'I wish to hear it again. Whilst you are about it, you had better tell all.'

'I had no intention of injuring her, Mr Walcheren; indeed, you must believe that! I told her all her father had commissioned me to say, and she laughed in my face at the idea. She wanted to know what business it was of mine to interfere in her affairs, and why her father had not gone down himself to make his proposals in person. And then, I was mad enough to tell her the reason that I took such an interest in all that concerned her. I told her how long I had loved her.'

'You insulted her, in fact,' exclaimed Frederick, making a step forward.

'No, Mr Walcheren, no,' cried the coward, cringing before him; 'I did not, upon my honour.'

'Your honour,' sneered the other.

'I did not insult her; indeed I thought too highly of her for that. But she goaded me on to saying what I did. And then she turned round on me with such bitter scorn that she drove me beside myself. She almost spurned me from her in her mocking pride, and I saw she was perilously near the edge of the cliff. I stretched out my hand and laid it on her arm to save her from falling backward. But she wrenched her wrist from my grasp, crying out, "You brute! You want to push me over the cliffs now, I suppose." Upon my soul, Mr Walcheren, I had never dreamt of such an awful thing before. But, as she said the words, I suppose the devil entered into me,—something did, at any rate—and I thought, "And if I do, no one will have you evermore. If *I* can never hope to call you mine, I can prevent Walcheren doing so." I was mad—I must have been mad—for I had loved her so dearly, ever since she was a little child, and yet, at that moment, I seemed to have but one wish —to see her out of the reach of everybody, even myself—to know she would be unable ever again to taunt me, or despise me, or laugh over my infatuation. So, without thinking of the consequences, I gave her a push backwards insteads of a pull forwards, and you know the rest. She fell—and I have never known a happy hour since. I don't think I shall ever have a happy hour again.'

' Not if I can help it!' replied Frederick, with emphasis.

Hindes started, and changed colour.

' But you cannot betray me. My reve-lation is sacred. You said yourself that the secrets of the confessional are inviol-ate.'

'I know I did. But *this* is not a confessional, Mr Hindes.'

The wretched man glared round him like a rat who has been trapped.

'Do you mean to say that you are not bound to keep secrets told *out* of the church?'

'A priest is bound to maintain utter silence on all matters revealed under the seal of confession, whether in the church or out of it, but you and I are in the position of two private individuals. You came to call on me like any other person; therefore, it lies in my discretionary power to keep what you have told me this evening to myself, or not.'

'My God!' cried Hindes, 'I am lost!'

Then the nerve which he had ruined by the use of morphia entirely forsook him, and he fell on his knees and crawled to the feet of the man he had so sorely wronged, like an abject animal.

'Mercy! mercy!' he groaned, 'don't visit my crime upon my head, for the sake of my poor wife and children. I loved her

'Silence, sir!' thundered Frederick, 'remember you are speaking of *my wife!* Mercy!' he continued, after a pause, 'what mercy did you have on me, when you cut my dream of love so cruelly short, and in so devilish a manner? What mercy had you on her, my sweet, innocent, loving Jenny, when your accursed hand hurled her over those awful rocks? My love! my darling!' he continued, pacing the floor of his room in his agitation, 'why was I not by your side at that fatal moment, that I might have made this fiend pay the penalty of his crime by sharing your fate? My wife—my wife—and he asks me to show mercy upon him!'

'Mr Walcheren! I will do anything—anything—if you will only keep my secret now. It can do you no good to publish it, nor *her* either. Let me go free and I will pay any penalty you like. I am a rich man. If your Church demands it, I will pay half my fortune into her coffers, or, if you wish it, I will sign a paper, promising to leave England at once—

to-morrow, if you insist upon it—and never show my face in the country again ; I will perform any penance you may put upon me, only don't make the matter public property after this length of time.'

He had forgotten, in his cowardly fear, that Walcheren had no witness against him, that his crime had been committed in secret, and that an English jury had acquitted him, and all men, from blame. His conscience had turned him into such a sorry poltroon that his memory had departed with his manliness. He grovelled before his opponent on the ground —he even attempted to kiss his feet, but Frederick Walcheren spurned him from him with his boot.

'Don't touch me, you brute!' he exclaimed, using involuntarily the very words poor Jenny had blurted forth in her indignation, 'your very lips are contamination! Once for all, I will *not* spare you. If you escape to the uttermost ends of the earth, I will pursue you there! You shall walk no longer among your fellow-men like a whited sepulchre. If I unfrock myself in order to obtain it, I will have my revenge!'

'I have tried to make amends,' groaned Henry Hindes, who was still upon his knees. 'I have not used the money Mr Crampton left to my son. It is all there; I intend to endow a church or an hospital with it. But it was *hers*. It more justly belongs to you; you shall have it, every farthing, with double interest, if you will only consider your intention again and contemplate how little good you will do yourself and others by carrying it out.'

'You would bribe me with money, you miserable cur!' replied Frederick, witheringly—'pay me for my wife's murder—satisfy my craving for revenge by so many pounds, shillings and pence! But you will find I am not such an usurer as you imagine. I have not been brought up to trade, and if I had, I should not trade in my heart's affections. Be silent! I will listen to no more from your accursed lips. You have said enough! Leave my pre-

sence ; but don't think to hide yourself from
me. I will leave the priesthood to-morrow
—I will leave the Church itself—I will
resign my hopes of salvation, if need be,
but you shall not go unpunished for this
hideous crime!'

So speaking, Frederick Walcheren left
the room suddenly, slamming the door after
him, whilst Henry Hindes remained on
the floor, with the tears running down his
cheeks. When he found himself alone,
he rose from his knees and slowly quitted
the apartment, not knowing what to do or
where to go, or whom to consult, on the unhappy position in which he found himself.

The young priest was still pacing the
floor of his dormitory, in the greatest dis-
quietude, when a lay brother appeared, to
tell him that a lady wished to speak to him
in the common parlour, where the clergy
usually receive their female visitors. Frederick tried to calm himself as he went down
to meet her, but he felt very unequal to
administering comfort, or giving advice to
anyone. But what was his relief, on enter-

ing the parlour, to find that his visitor was Rhoda Berry. She was robed all in black, and looked so quiet and graceful that he was not surprised that the brother had called her a lady. Half his care seemed to fall off his shoulders as he recognised her.

'Oh! Rhoda,' he exclaimed, coming forward eagerly to greet her, 'how good it is of you to answer my appeal so soon. Were you surprised that I should wish to see you again? I am in great trouble, and I long for your advice and counsel. You were always giving me good advice in the old days, Rhoda, so you must do the same now.'

'Certainly, if I can,' replied the girl, in an astonished tone; 'but what advice of mine can benefit you, now that you are a priest, so high above me and so far, far away?'

'Do you think I must necessarily be so high above you, Rhoda, just because I have been ordained,' said Frederick, sadly. 'I, on the contrary, have but lately found out that I am lower than I even believed myself to be; full of the old worldliness, the old envy, malice and all uncharitableness.'

'I don't believe it,' replied Rhoda, stoutly, 'you were never anything like that, Fred— I beg your pardon, I meant Mr Wal- cheren—'

'Nonsense! call me Fred, Rhoda. What else should I be to you than that?'

'But *now*—' said Rhoda, dubiously, 'it sounds so disrespectful.'

'Does it? Never mind. It eases my heart to hear it. I feel very much alone sometimes, Rhoda, and as if I had isolated myself from all who loved me.'

'I suppose you do, but perhaps the feel- ing will wear off with time. But I do not like to hear you accuse yourself of faults of which you were never guilty. I am sure you were never either envious or malicious. You were always the most kind-hearted and generous of men, at least to me. So I am sure you cannot have become uncharitable now.'

'Perhaps I have had more cause lately to bring my bad qualities into play. I have had a great shock, the last week, Rhoda! I have discovered that my dear wife did not meet ber death by an accident, but was foully murdered.'

The girl sprung from her seat with a genuine exclamation of horror.

The dead woman had been more than her rival. She had actually ousted her from her lover's affections, and she had had many bitter and envious thoughts about them both. But, when she heard that she had been murdered, all her resentment vanished in a flood of pity so vast, that she felt, at that moment, as if she would have laid down her own life to bring her back again. And how she pitied *him* too—her poor lover, whose infidelity to herself had met with so terrible an ending.

' Oh ! my poor, poor boy !' she cried, forgetful of his priesthood and everything, except that once he had been her own ; ' how sorry I am for you. How did you hear it ? Who did the awful deed ? What reason could anyone have had to injure you so fearfully ? '

And then the tender-hearted girl sat down in her chair again and burst into tears—partly for poor dead Jenny, and partly for herself.

'I knew you would feel for me,' replied Frederick. 'You have been a good friend to me all along. I cannot answer all your questions. If I could, I should not have need of your advice. But listen to me, and I will tell you the whole story.'

He drew a chair opposite to her on the other side of the table, and leaned his arms across it.

'You have heard of the confessional, Rhoda, where Catholics tells their sins to a priest, and, when truly penitent, receive absolution. Last Saturday week, Father Henniker, one of our priests, was ill, and I was ordered to take his place in the confessional, and as the people who confess cannot see the face of the confessor, no one knew but that Father Henniker was in his usual place. Do you understand?'

'Perfectly!'

'Whilst I was engaged thus, a man entered the confessional, and, to my horror and amazement, told me the whole history of my darling wife's—You don't mind my calling her that before you, do you, Rhoda?'

'No, no; call her just what you like. I should not love you—I mean, I should not *have* loved you—Fred, if you had married her without caring for her.'

'I did you an injustice by the question. You are too true-hearted a woman to mind it. Well, this man related the whole dreadful story to me, and told me that he had killed her himself—that she had not fallen over the cliffs by mistake, but that he had pushed her over—the villain!—on purpose, and with the design of killing her!'

'Oh, Fred, what did you do?' exclaimed Rhoda, with her blue eyes opened to their widest extent.

'My dear, I could do nothing. That was the terrible part of it. I had to sit there and listen to the account of his villainy and make no sign. But, as he left the confessional, I opened the half door on my side and showed my face, and he looked as though the heavens had opened to rain down judgment on him.'

'You knew the man, then, and he knew you,' said Rhoda.

'Yes! but I am bound by the most solemn oaths not to tell the name nor communications of any penitent who confesses to me. Oh! Rhoda, pity me! You can fancy what I felt, cooped up there, and compelled to listen to perhaps a dozen more confessions, without the slightest idea of what they were all saying. I think some of them must have been rather astonished to have been let off so easily, for I absolved the whole lot without a murmur. All I could think of was how I could escape and take counsel of someone. My head and my heart were on fire! Had I followed my natural inclination, I should have rushed down the aisle after the brute and seized him by the throat, and squeezed his life out of him then and there. But I had to wait till I was set at liberty, and then I rushed to Father Tasker, an old friend of mine, and asked him what I ought to do about it.'

' And he told you—? '

' That I could do nothing, that, by reason
of my office, I must sit down like a dummy,
and let this murderer walk about the world
scot-free. That I must pray and hope, and
trust that someone else might bring him to
justice, or try and persuade him to confess
his crime to the law, but failing, this, I
could do nothing but be patient under my
heinous wrongs. *Patient!* when my beautiful girl lies in her grave, murdered, in the
spring-time of her youth, by a jealous brute
who could not bear to see our happiness;
when my married bliss has been cut short,
and all my earthly hopes shattered for ever;
when I have pledged myself, in my despair,
to be quiescent and forego my revenge.
Rhoda! it has nearly driven me mad! I feel
like that poor husband, of whom we read
during the Indian mutinies, who was bound
with cords whilst his lovely young wife was
outraged and murdered before his eyes, the
while the foam and blood dropped from his
mouth in his rage and agony. Here am I,
chained—bound—helpless, and all through

my own folly. I cannot bear it! I cannot
—I cannot!'

'Hush! hush, dear Fred, some one will
hear you!' exclaimed the girl, cautiously,
as she rose and listened at the door. 'I believe there is somebody in the passage now.
Cannot I see you somewhere else, in order
to talk over this unhappy business? May
you not leave this place?'

'Certainly! I am free to go and come as
I choose. Where are you staying in town?'

'At my old address. The landlady knows
me, and is very kind. I do not intend to
remain over to-morrow, unless you want
me. You see, I have to leave the—the—
little one with mother, and he is getting
rather troublesome now.'

'Is he quite well?' inquired Frederick,
wistfully.

'Yes; but can you come and see me to-
night?'

'I can, and I will, at seven o'clock. Till
then, good-bye.'

And he let her cautiously out of the front
door.

CHAPTER VIII.

THE young priest was punctual to his appointment, and found Rhoda ready to receive him. She was alone, and in the room where they had so often met before, yet she displayed no self-consciousness of the fact. It was evident that she had accepted the position, in which they now stood to one another, as final. Frederick Walcheren a priest was as dead to her as if he lay in his grave. She saw in him only a friend, whom she had once dearly loved and trusted in, to be advised, comforted and maybe led aright. Had she been a Catholic, this state of mind would not have been extraordinary on her part, since, for a Catholic to think of a priest otherwise than a priest, would be sacrilege. But Rhoda was a Protestant, who had been brought up to detest Popery, and everything connected with it, so that the reverential attitude she now assumed towards her former lover was due, not to his Church, but himself. She cared nothing, individually, for his office, but she still cared too much for him to tempt him to say a word, or do an act, which should become a reproach to him. She rose as he entered, but did not even hold out her hand in greeting. All the courtesy she extended, was to ask him if he would like a cup of tea after his walk.

'Thanks, Rhoda,' he replied; 'I think it would be very refreshing, for I have just come off a long round of visits. The women of the poorer classes I can see at any time, but it is only in the evenings that I can catch the men.'

'But there is not nearly so much trouble to induce the men to go to church in your religion as there is in ours, or so I have heard,' said the girl, as she busied herself with the kettle and the teapot.

'No, I suppose not, because they are reared from infancy to believe that it is a mortal sin not to attend Mass once on a

Sunday. And a mortal sin, unconfessed, means, with us, eternal damnation. But what is the use, Rhoda, of a duty performed under such a dread? If it is only done from fear of hell, it may as well not be done at all.

'We have not met to-night to discuss religion,' said Rhoda, as she placed his cup of tea before him, 'and you would never convert me if we had. You may remember that was one of the matters we used to argue about in the past, and finally agreed that each of us was to have our own way. But I quite agree with you, that a duty performed from the fear of man's opinion, or of future punishment, is just worth nothing in the eyes of God. There is only one person we have to please, or to account for our actions to, and that is Himself.'

'You used not to think so much of God when I first knew you, Rhoda,' said Frederick, 'or, at all events, I do not remember ever hearing you speak of Him.'

The tears filled Rhoda's eyes.

'No, perhaps not. But things that have happened since then may have drawn my

thoughts more that way. You must feel
yourself, Fred, that when one knows
trouble and loss, one naturally goes to
Heaven for comfort. It has been the
same with you. That is why people say
that it is sent to turn us to God.'

'Yes, for such as I, perhaps, Rhoda, who
was so selfishly absorbed in my own joy
as to forget the unhappiness I caused to
others—I seemed to have no resource but
to devote the rest of my life to Heaven.
But you are young, and your loss has not
been like mine! I have had to give up a
wife who was far too good for me, whilst
you lost only a most worthless friend, un-
worthy of the name, who did his best to
ensure your destruction with his own.'

'Let us talk of what we were doing this
afternoon,' responded the girl, quietly. 'I
have thought of nothing else since we
parted. It is so dreadful, so very, very
sad ; so terrible for you to hear so suddenly,
and when you had no idea of such a thing.
You told me that you had applied for
counsel to your fellow-priests, and all they

could advise you was to have patience.
Patience for *what*, Frederick ? '

'For nothing, Rhoda. Patience to see
the murderer of my poor wife walking
about the world as usual, beloved by his
family, respected by his friends, and honoured by his fellow-men. That is all. I
may live for the next fifty years—so may
he—eating my heart out to know my great
wrong goes unavenged, and pacifying myself with prayer the while—prayer that my
enemy may find grace hereafter, I suppose,
as well as here.'

'Fred,' said Rhoda, leaning her elbows
on the table opposite to him, and looking
him steadily in the face, 'if you had your
whole will in this matter, what would
you do ? '

'Hang the brute fifty times, and gloat
over his agony all the while.'

'Oh, no, you wouldn't,' she replied,
shaking her head.

'I would, Rhoda, I would. What !
spare him who had no mercy on my lost
darling ? You do not know me.'

' I think I do, better than you know yourself. You feel like that now, certainly, but
when it came to actually *doing* it, you
would draw back and say, " This is not
my work. Leave him to God." '

' And let my darling lie in her bloody
grave unavenged? Never ! '

' Is she not avenged? You have described to me what an abject, trembling,
miserable object her murderer is ! Do you
suppose he has not suffered such tortures
of remorse as would make the gallows a
welcome relief to him ? There is no hell,
Frederick, like that which we carry within
ourselves — the worm that dieth not.
Leave this wretched man to his own
remorse ! That will prove a greater hell
to him than the hangman's rope, and be a
jewel in your heavenly crown.'

' But *why* should I do this, Rhoda ? I
can understand the priests telling me I
must forego my revenge because I must
not violate the secrets of the confessional,
yet, even they said that, if the confession
were made to me in private, as it was this

afternoon, it would be legitimate for me to
bring the criminal to justice.   But you say
just the opposite.   Why ? '

' Because I am not speaking according
to any formula, Frederick, of what the
Church will, or will not, permit you to do.
I am talking to you as a friend who thinks
only of your individual good, and nothing
of what people or Churches will say.   I am
thinking only of how God will view the
matter, and what He might say when you
had brought this murderer to earthly justice.
" Well ! and now that you are satisfied with
regard to him who robbed you, how about
yourself ?   Have *you* never robbed your
neighbour ?   Have *you* murdered no good
thing which he prized ?—never taken from
him anything which you can never give
back again ?   Is there no murder but that
of the mortal life ? "   Oh ! Fred, I do not
mean or wish to reproach you, but I want
you to consider your own past life—your
life and mine—and see if we are not liable
to make amends in the sight of God as
well as our fellow-creatures—even this poor

murderer, on whom you thirst to take your revenge.'

The young man had hidden his face in his hands as she spoke to him, and, for a few moments, was too absorbed in thought to answer her. Here was what the world would have called his victim—the girl he had betrayed under a promise of eternal fidelity—who had trusted in him and been deceived—who had never blamed nor reproached him, but accepted her sad fate in all humility, teaching him true Christianity as no one had ever taught him before.

He had robbed her of her good name and her virtue. He had murdered her belief and faith in him. He had taken from her that which he could never restore —her spotless reputation, and her pride in herself. He had left her to support her shame and sorrow alone—the reproaches of her family, the scorn of her companions— whilst he had been revelling in Jenny's beauty and Jenny's love, and mourning over her death and his own exceeding loss.

Yet, Rhoda had forgiven him in the divinest manner. She had felt with him in his sorrow, but never asked him to share hers. She had listened, with all sympathy to his tale of misery, but never once alluded to her own. She had been a true friend to him in all things, and, if his life could do her any good, he owed it to her ; and then, with a deep groan, he came back to himself and remembered that he was dead to the world ; he could benefit no one in it any more ; he had made himself a cipher, a machine, an automaton, to be moved only by the will of others, and never to think or act for himself. The groan alarmed Rhoda. She feared she had said too much.

'Forgive me, she said softly, 'if I was over bold. I forgot, for the moment, what a gulf there is between us, and fancied I was scolding you as of yore. You will not think too much of what I said. It is only a girl's opinion, after all, and you should know so much better than I.'

'Yes, *should*,' echoed Frederick Wal

cheren, moodily ; ' but the question is if I
do! Don't blame yourself, Rhoda. You
have put things in a new light before me,
and I thank you for it. I will go home
and think over the matter again. After
all, you are right! What real good would
this man's swinging do me ? It cannot
restore my murdered wife nor my own
peace of mind. I should be none the
better for it.'

' I am sure you would not, and especially if you had been the means of bringing
him to justice. It would only add another
link to your chain of sorrow. Besides,
Fred, it would cast, as it were, a blot on
your ministry. I feel shy of touching on
such a delicate subject, but you will stand
even this, I know, coming from me. The
first fault, my dear, was your own. Had
you not married that young lady without
the consent of her parents, she would never
have been placed in so dangerous a
position. This man would not have
followed her, and she would have had no
chance of enraging him. There have been

faults on all sides. How can you tell, if you had been placed under the same circumstances as this wretched murderer, whether you might not stand at this moment in the same position? You know I am not attempting to defend him. His crime excites the greatest abhorrence in my eyes, especially as it has so cruelly hurt you. But I cannot help feeling the same about all murderers—that, but for God's grace, we might have encountered the same lot. How many hasty blows are given how many more intended — anyone of which might, if dealt a few inches nearer or farther, cause death instead of mere pain. You say this man told you that his life had been a curse to him ever since—that he was in despair. Is that not sufficient punishment for his sin? What can be more terrible than a life of remorse? The gallows would be preferable a thousand times over. Don't try to hurry him out of the world before he has repented and tried to make such amends as may be in his power. Perhaps God may send the thought to him. Perhaps your leniency may have the same effect! At anyrate, Fred, whatever may be his ultimate fate, don't *you* have a hand in it! *Don't*, for the sake of the old days!'

The tears were standing in her bright eyes as she leaned across the table and put her hand upon his arm. He placed his own hand over it.

'Were the old days very dear to you, Rhoda?' he asked.

'You know they were, but it is of no use talking of it. Since your lot in life is fixed, it would be foolish to revert to the time when you thought otherwise from now. I hear your voice, and fancy I have got my old friend again, but, when I look at you, dressed in that strange manner, and with your beautiful brown hair cropped off, I can hardly believe you are the same Fred I knew. And it is best so, is it not?'

'But what I am afraid of, Rhoda, is that my face and clothes are the only things that are changed about me. That is one thing I wanted to talk to you about. I fear I have made a terrible mistake in becoming a priest. You see, this time last year, I was so mad with grief, the shock I experienced had so shattered my nerves, that I was not myself. All I wanted was to find forgetfulness, even at the sacrifice of worldly good. My friends and relations worked largely on my frame of mind, by assuring me the peace I longed for was to be found only in the Church. My mother and godfather had intended me for that profession, and I was in too despondent a state of mind to care what they did with me, or made of me. So I drifted into ordination, not from a love of God, but of despairing grief for my great loss. And now, I am sure, I am unfitted for it. I am not nearly good enough. My thoughts and desires are all with the world I have left. I have no vocation for the ministry. What am I to do? Tell me, Rhoda. I have faith in your sincerity and purity of teaching. Don't consider anything, except

how I can please Heaven best. I don't
want to please myself so much, as not to
disgrace my calling.'

'If you ask my advice, Fred, I can only
give it in the words of your favourite
Shakespeare :—

" To thine own self, be true !
It follows, as the night the day,
Thou canst not then be false to any man." '

'Be true to myself!' mused Frederick
Walcheren. 'Yes, Rhoda, you are right!
That must be the only true test of any
man's conduct.'

'Be true to the divinity that is in you,
Fred. If *you* feel—if your soul—your
very self feels that you will live an
honester and better life by leaving the
Church—a life nearer God, and more in
accordance with the nature which He has
given you—then don't go by what any
priest, or Church, or law says, but be a
law to yourself—and act like not only a
Christian, but *a man*, with free thoughts,
and free aspirations, and a God-given right

to regulate his own life as he may see best for himself and others.'

'Oh, you little heretic!' said Frederick, laughing, 'what would they have done to you a few centuries ago if you had been overheard uttering such blasphemies! You would have been condemned to be burnt at the stake!'

'Should I?' retorted Rhoda. 'Well, I should not think much of a religion that could do that!'

'They both did it,' replied Frederick, 'the Protestants as well as the Catholics! Everyone who differed from them in opinion, had to pay the penalty of their rashness.'

'Then I shouldn't have thought much of either of them,' said the girl. 'Fred! religion was meant to bring us nearer God, not farther from Him. The Church is not God, the priests are not God, the Bible, prayer—all these—are only so many helps to bring us nearer Him. Why think about what *they* will say then. Think only what God will say, and He speaks to you

through your own conscience, and not
through your fellow-men.'

'Rhoda, you astound me,' exclaimed
her companion; 'where have you learned
all this wisdom? You used not to talk
to me like this when we knew each
other before. Who has taught you so
much? With whom have you been as-
sociating?'

The girl looked down and reddened.

'With no one but myself,' she answered
gently. 'I have been very much alone.
You see, I have been too much ashamed to
go amongst the other girls. But I think I
have learned a great deal from my little
baby. He came, you know, Fred, when I
was so very unhappy and despairing, and
he seemed like a little messenger of God
to me, so sweet and innocent and sinless,
and yet, all mine, who was so wicked and
ungrateful and repining. I suppose I
ought to have been very much ashamed
of him, but I never was. He seemed to
say to me, when he looked up in my face
and smiled, whilst I was weeping over

him : "Yes, you have been very wicked, and you are very unhappy, but here I am, you see, sent straight from God to comfort you. And, if you will be good for the future, He will let me stay to make up to you for all you have lost." It was silly of me, wasn't it? to fancy such things, but they comforted me, and so I go on fancying them, even to this day. And baby has seemed to make me think of God and bring me nearer to Him than I have ever been before. And oh! Fred,' she continued, bursting out into a sudden enthusiasm, which she had never permitted herself to exhibit before, 'he is such a darling little creature, you can't think, so fat and strong, and he can toddle all over the place by himself. He was fourteen months old yesterday. But I forgot,' said Rhoda, suddenly checking herself; 'I oughtn't to mention him to you now. It will hurt you to remember it. Please forgive me, Fred. I should not have done it. It was a mistake.'

She looked at him, and, to her pity and

surprise, saw that tears were standing in his eyes.

'Talk to me just as you will, Rhoda,' he said, 'I love to hear you.   How can I say I am glad you have this little child to comfort you, when I remember all the shame and sorrow he has brought you, and of which I am the cause ?   Yet, perhaps, God knows best, and sent him with a holy purpose.   May He bless you both, and reward you for your sweet, womanly goodness to me.   I cannot.   Will you tell me some more about him ?' he added, humbly.

'Why, yes, of course, Fred, if you care to hear it!   But mother says, if I once begin talking of my black crow, as she calls him, I never stop.'

'Is he so very dark, then ?' asked the young man, gazing at the girl's golden hair.

'Oh! yes, not a bit like me, thank goodness!   His eyes are like black velvet, and so is his hair.   I am glad of that. He reminds me of you!   And he has six teeth, and eats crusts like anything ! And he can say "muvver" and "danny" quite well !'

'Nothing else?' inquired Frederick, wistfully.

'Only "sugar," replied Rhoda, looking at him as much as to say, 'How can I teach him of a father he will never know?'

'And your mother,' continued Walcheren, 'did she pronounce Anathema Maranatha on me, Rhoda, for the shabby trick I played you?'

'She was very, very angry at first, Fred. She could hardly help being that; but she has been an angel of goodness to me all through. And she is really very fond of Freddy, now!'

'You called him after me!' cried the young man, eagerly.

'Was I wrong? Are you angry?' said Rhoda, colouring from cheek to brow.

'Angry! No! why should I be, only you might have called the poor bantling after a better man.'

'*I* did not think so,' said Rhoda, simply.

There was a long pause between them before the young man rose to take his leave. How strange it seemed that, all at once, he had become timid in the presence of this young girl who had such faith in him. They had been so much to each other, and now they were so little; such a wide gulf separated their interests and lives. And yet there was one tiny link between them which neither could ever forget.

'It is getting late! I must go,' said Frederick, as he stood up and held out his hand to her.

Rhoda took it in a lifeless manner. She dared not press it—it was the hand of a priest, not of her lover. Yet, not to press it, and when he was in trouble, seemed so hard. But she dropped it instead, as if her own had no power to retain it.

'Good-night!' she murmured. 'God bless you, Frederick, and help you out of this new trouble. I shall go back to Luton by the first train to-morrow.'

He longed to say 'Don't,' but he dared not. Whatever lay in the future for him, he must not say a word more than necessary to her, whilst he wore those robes. So he said 'Good-night!' also, in an awkward manner, as if he were ashamed to part with her so coldly, and turned away. But, as he reached the door, he halted for a moment to add,—'You have done me so much good, I feel quite hopeful since I have seen you! God bless you!' and, nodding kindly, went his way.

And when he had disappeared, Rhoda sank down on her knees, and thanked God that she had seen him again, and that he still thought of and regarded her as a friend.

CHAPTER IX.

When Henry Hindes left the presence of Frederick Walcheren, he hailed a hansom and ordered the driver to take him back to Hampstead. He was not only unable to stand or walk, he was incapable of thinking. He lolled back in the hansom like a dead body, and had barely strength to alight at his own door. The servant who admitted him, used as he had been to see his master look ill of late, ran down to the lower regions to say that he believed 'The guv'ner was dying, he seemed that bad.' Hannah, who, having heard his entrance, came smiling out into the hall to meet him, was struck by his altered appearance, and exclaimed,—

'What is the matter with you? Have you been ill? Are you in any pain?'

To all which, Hindes only said in answer,—

'Be quiet! Hold your tongue! Am I destined never to have any peace?'

He pushed his way past her to the library, where she followed him.

'How can you be so unkind and ungrateful, Henry? I was coming to tell you a piece of good news, that I knew you would be glad to hear.'

'Good news! What good news can there ever be for me again?'

'I believe you will think it the very best you could receive. Doctor Sewell has been here this afternoon, and brought Mr Lyndhurst with him. They made a thorough examination of Wally, and Mr Lyndhurst says we may set our minds completely at rest with regard to his spine being permanently affected. It received a great shock by the concussion, but all the dangerous symptoms have abated, and I am to let him get up for a few hours to-morrow, and so gradually put him on his feet again. Now, isn't that good news?'

Hannah said sweetly, as she put her hand upon her husband's arm.

But Hindes did not smile, nor look at her. He jerked his arm roughly from her detaining clasp instead, and, sinking down upon a sofa, murmured,—

'Too late! too late!'

'Too late!' exclaimed his wife, in a tone of surprise, 'what do you mean, Henry? Too late to have our dear child restored to us, safe and sound again. I thought that was what you were praying for, with myself. I thought the news would make you wild with joy. What are you thinking of?'

'Just what I say! I am thankful for the child's sake, of course, but the news comes too late for me. My secret is known, Hannah! I have betrayed myself. The bloodhounds of justice are on my track.'

'Good God!' she said under her breath, 'how did it happen? To whom did you speak? What made you do it?'

'My evil genius, I suppose,' replied Hindes, grovelling on the sofa. 'I could not bear the misery and the suspense any longer. It was burning into my soul like a red-hot iron, and I thought, if I confessed it, I might find consolation. So I went into a Roman Catholic confessional one day last week, and told my story to the priest. And who do you suppose he turned out to be?'

'How can I tell? I know no priests.'

'Frederick Walcheren!'

'Frederick Walcheren!' cried his wife; 'but how came he to be in a confessional?'

'He *is* a priest! He entered the Church, it seems, after—after—you know what! And I happened to enter his confessional! Was it not the irony of Fate? The finger of Heaven, or the devil tracking me to my destruction?'

'But, Henry, the secrets of the confessional are sacred! I know so much! It was most unfortunate that you should have committed such an error as to confess your sin to *him*. But he cannot make any use of his knowledge. So far, you are safe!'

'But that is not the worst of it, Hannah! He recognised my voice and, as I was leav-

ing the accursed place, he showed his face
at the open door.   It made me dread the
worst.   I thought he might find means to
let others learn what he had, or perhaps
reveal it altogether.   You never know
what these Roman Catholics may do.
They have no honour!'

'Don't blame others, Henry,' interposed
Hannah, gently, 'whilst you are blame-
worthy yourself.   Remember how deeply
you have wronged this man.   Yet, Mr
Walcheren was always a gentleman and a
man of honour, and I do not believe he
would reveal a secret, however terrible,
that had come to his knowledge through
such a channel.'

'I wish I had thought the same.   I wish
I had consulted you before,' groaned her
husband, 'but I feared the worst, and it
weighed so on my mind that I determined
to visit him privately, and learn what he
intended to do.   When I asked him, he
said, as you do, that he was forbidden, under
the most heavy penalties, to repeat anything that he might hear during his office

as confessor. If I had only been content with that. But his manner made me feel secure, and I wanted to make myself look as little guilty as possible in his eyes, so I told him the story over again, and then—'

'Well, what then, Henry? Was there any harm in that?' inquired Hannah.

'I have d—d myself by it, that's all!' exclaimed Hindes, despairingly. 'I had hardly finished when he told me that, although secrets told under the seal of confession were inviolate, we were not in a confessional at that moment, and it lay within his discretionary powers to make what use of my revelation he chose.'

'Oh! Henry, Henry!' cried Hannah, 'what have you done? What misery and disgrace have you not brought upon us all?'

'Yes, that's right,' he answered roughly; think of the children and yourself before me. And it's all your fault, from beginning to end. Who was it urged me to confess my sins and obtain forgiveness for them? Who was it said that, if I humiliated myself, Heaven might have mercy on Wally and give us back his health in exchange?'

'And so He has!' said Hannah, joyfully. 'He *has* accepted the painful effort you have made, Henry, and rewarded it by giving us this fresh hope of the boy's recovery. Oh! my poor husband! have I been harsh to you? I did not mean it! I was only shocked to think of the danger you ran! But have no fear, dearest! I feel sure that God, who put it into your heart to confess, will not let it lead you to public disgrace. Frederick Walcheren will not betray your secret. I am sure of it! Let *me* go to him, Henry, and plead to him for mercy and forbearance in the name of myself and my little children. I feel certain he will not refuse me, if it were only for dear Jenny's sake, and my great love for her.'

'No, no!' said Hindes, hoarsely; 'you must do no such thing! You don't know him. He would spurn you from him. A woman cannot realise a man's feelings in such a matter. He loved her—he must feel like a wild beast deprived of his prey. He would tread on you, or anyone who stood in his path. He is thirsting for his revenge! He told me so, and when I craved him for mercy in your name and the children's, he only asked what mercy I had shown him. Hannah! it is useless to ignore the fact. My doom is fixed! If it is not the gallows, it is public and utter disgrace.'

All the woman rose in Hannah's breast at these words, and the man before her was one to be protected and solaced and thought for.

'It shall be neither, my dearest,' she answered firmly; 'only trust to me. I have pondered over the difficulties that might happen in your case, Henry, and I think I have found a way out of them. You are tired and worn out with misery and suspense, my poor love. Let me think for you. You must go to your room now, and try to rest. I will bring you some dinner myself, for you mustn't let the servants see you in this state. I

will sit up to-night, and get your clothes
ready, and pack your portmanteau, and
to-morrow, instead of going to the city,
you shall take the train for Liverpool, and
the first steamer for the Argentine Re-
public. *There* you will be safe from English laws, and pursuit will be useless. As
soon as you are fairly off, I will wind up
your affairs, and join you with the children. Trust everything to me. Only
look after your own safety.'

Henry Hindes raised his tear-stained
face from the sofa cushions, and stared at
his wife.

' *You !* ' he exclaimed, wonderingly.
' *You* will undertake to do all this ? But
you have never been used to business in
your life, Hannah. How do you propose
to take such a burden on your shoulders,
and to accomplish it ? '

' My love for you will teach me, Henry,'
she said simply. ' Besides, do not think
I am so presumptuous as to suppose I can
do it all by myself. My uncle, Bailey, is
an excellent man of business, remember,

and our solicitor will help me. The business may be sold something under value, perhaps, but I promise I will consent to nothing rash, and all I shall strive for is to realise the bulk of your money, and transmit it to you in the Argentine, that you may make a home for me and the children there.'

'But it will be exile for life, Hannah. I shall never be able to show my face in England again, remember.'

'I only remember that I would rather spend the rest of my life in the desert with you, Henry, than live without you anywhere,' replied Hannah, with a watery smile.

'And you can feel thus for *me*—a murderer!' said Hindes, wonderingly.

But she laid her hand upon his mouth.

'I will not let you call yourself by that name, Henry,' she said. 'I never think of you as such. I begin to believe, as you have sometimes told me, that it was the effects of an unfortunate accident.'

'God bless you! God bless you!'

cried the wretched man, bursting into tears, as she took him in her arms and laid his weary head upon her faithful bosom.

They talked over the plan she had suggested a little longer, and then Hannah persuaded him to take some refreshment and to go upstairs to his own room and rest. But, left alone again, all his fears returned. The presence of his wife had a magnetic effect upon him, but, as soon as she had withdrawn, he became a prey to the phantoms raised by his uneasy conscience. He could not rest in his bed, but kept starting up, fancying that he heard voices in the hall, or on the stairs, people inquiring for him, demanding to see and speak with him, forcing their way up to his bedroom, whilst Hannah tried in vain to bar their ingress.

She, on the contrary, though feeling a little nervous and uneasy at the story her husband had brought home, fancied she saw a happier future before them than she had dared to hope for. It was better for them all, she thought, that matters had come to a crisis, and they were compelled to leave the country, where they could never again live in any comfort.

Once Henry was out of England, she would seek an interview with Mr Walcheren, and ask his forbearance for the sake of her poor children, who would have their innocent lives stained by the publicity of their father's crime. Once her husband was safe, she was sure she could arrange everything to her own satisfaction, and, when she joined him, they would begin a new life, unshadowed by fear or deceit.

She sat down quite cheerfully to her dinner, at which the master so seldom appeared now that his absence was nothing remarkable, and succeeded in making the attendants think that there was nothing more wrong than usual. After dinner, she carried a cup of coffee up to her husband with her own hands, but found him in an unaccountably nervous condition, considering how hopeful he had been when she parted with him.

'Who is that downstairs?' he asked, glancing fearfully at the door by which she had entered, as if he thought some-one would steal in after her. 'I heard voices. Whom have you been talking to?'

'No one, dear, except the servants,' re-plied his wife. 'I met Ellen on the stairs just now coming from Wally's room, and she says the little rogue is so free from pain to-night that he has been romping over the bed.'

'No, no! Not that!' replied Hindes, fretfully. 'There was someone else. Don't try to deceive me. A man's voice. I heard it distinctly.'

'Why should I deceive you, Henry?' said Hannah, mildly. 'I assure you, you are mistaken. I have been quite alone since you came upstairs.'

'I don't believe it! You're lying to me!' he answered, glaring at her with demoniacal eyes.

She was used to his vagaries, and found it best not to argue against them. So she put the bedclothes over him carefully again, and, stooping down, kissed him, and bade him go to sleep.

'I shall come up very early to-night, you know, dear, in order to arrange your things, and, if you wish it, I will rouse you then, but it will be much better if you will try and sleep. You said just now, you know, that you would be good, and let me manage everything for you—and so I will. Only try and rest, for you will have so much fatigue to-morrow.'

Her soothing had its usual effect on him, and he lay down and closed his eyes, and murmured something about not deserving to have so good a wife, which was eminently true.

Hannah occupied herself a little about the adjoining apartment, until she thought he had dropped off again, and then went softly downstairs again. What was her amazement to be met at the foot by one of her servants, with the intelligence that a gentleman was waiting in the drawing-room to see her.

'A gentleman!' she echoed; 'what is his name, James?'

'He did not give his name, ma'am. He asked for the master first, but I said I thought he had gone up to bed, and then he said he would wait and see. I think he's some sort of a priest, if you please, ma'am; at least, he looks like it.'

Some sort of a priest! Hannah's heart stood still at the words, but she resolved to know what he came for. Perhaps it was Frederick Walcheren himself, and, in that case, she would plead her own cause to him. Without a moment's delay, she passed down the corridor, and entered the drawing-room. It *was* Walcheren who stood before her! Altered as he was by his dress, and the terrible experience he had passed through, she recognised him at once. But he seemed rather taken aback at her appearance. He had evidently not expected to see her, and he neither came forward to meet her nor offered his hand. As for Hannah, she stood trembling before him, as if he had been a judge.

'Mrs Hindes, I believe,' began Frederick, courteously, 'but I am sorry they troubled you, madam. It was your husband I came to see. I have a little business with him.'

'Yes, yes, I know. He has told me,' replied poor Hannah. 'We have no secrets from each other, Mr Walcheren, and Henry has related to me the whole account of his seeing you in the confessional and visiting you at your private residence afterwards.'

'He has told you his motives and what has passed between us?' said the young man, in astonishment.

'Everything, sir, and I have known it from the beginning. Oh, Mr Walcheren,' she went on rapidly, 'I was going to see you about it. I wanted to plead to you for mercy for my poor children and myself. I have no excuses to make for my unhappy husband. How could I have, when Jenny'—here Hannah's tears commenced to flow and her utterance became choked with her sobs—'when she was my very, very dearest friend? No one mourned her loss more than I did, and to think—to think— But my wretched husband has lived in hell since that miserable day. He has never known one happy moment. If any man ever repented a sin, he has done his. Can you not find it in your heart, Mr Walcheren, to show him a little mercy? It would be very noble of you if you would. Henry shall never annoy you by his presence again. We are intending to leave the country, never to return. Only, if you could find it in your heart to spare him—to forgive as you hope to be forgiven —for the sake of his little children, sir—'

She attempted to fall at his feet, but he raised her.

'Mrs Hindes, you greatly distress me,' he said. 'I did not expect, nor wish to see you when I came here to-night. I had but one object in doing so—'

'Yes, yes,' she interposed, 'I know it. To tell him to prepare for the worst— to say you must, in justice to yourself and *her* dear memory, let the law take its course—and if you had only waited a few days, I should have got him out of your reach.'

'But, indeed, you are mistaken,' replied Walcheren, 'that was not my intention. Of course, I don't pretend to deny the awful feelings for revenge which his story evoked in my breast against him. I loved —I loved *her* very dearly, Mrs Hindes—'

'Oh, my darling, my darling,' broke out Hannah.

'And you loved her too,' he proceeded, tenderly, 'and must understand what I felt on first hearing the awful story of her death. But that was my first impression. I have reflected since—a friend of mine has been probing my heart and motives for me, and setting things generally in a clearer light, and the conclusion I have arrived at is, that I shall do nothing more in the matter. I will bury my resentment in my lost wife's grave, and, though you must feel that I could never see, nor speak to your husband again, yet he is safe from me. His secret is also safe, as far as I am concerned. My lips shall never dis-

close it. I came here to-night to tell
him so.'

'How—how can we ever thank you,'
whispered Hannah, through her tears.

'Your thanks are not due to me, but to
my friend. If she had not led my thoughts
the right way, they would not have gone
there by themselves. Set your mind at
rest, therefore, Mrs Hindes. The matter
is done with. Will you tell your husband
so from me?'

'Oh! gladly, thankfully, Mr Walcheren.
You have saved him. You have saved
us all. May God bless you and your friend
for it!'

'Thank you,' he returned quietly, as he
bowed and walked out into the hall.

Hannah followed him there.

'Do you go back by the station?' she
inquired. 'May I send you home in the
carriage?'

'No thank you! he answered, shudder-
ing at the idea of using anything that
belonged to Henry Hindes. 'I am a
poor man now, and not used to such

luxuries.   The   station   will   suit   me best.'

And then, without any greeting less formal than an inclination of his head, Frederick Walcheren passed out of the hall door and went on his way.   Hannah guessed the reason.   Dearly as she had loved the dead girl, he could not persuade himself to shake hands with the wife of her murderer.   Perhaps it was best so.   Frederick Walcheren would now pass out of their lives for ever.

Henry Hindes, with his ears quickened by fear, had heard the opening and shutting of the front door, and the slight conversation passing in the hall.   He had sprung out of his bed to listen, and crouched behind his bedroom door.   He had recognised Frederick Walcheren's voice, and caught the word 'station' twice repeated. Why had he come?   What was he there for?   And what 'station' could he be speaking off?   There was but one solution of the mystery in the morbid ideas of Henry   Hindes.   The   conscience   that

makes cowards of us all, had transformed
him into a trembling poltroon, incapable
of judging or arguing. Frederick Walcheren was in The Old Hall, and there
could be but one reason for his coming
there — to publicly denounce him as a
murderer — to have him arrested and
dragged to prison—to pursue him until
he landed him on the scaffold, and saw the
rope pulled that should hang him by the
neck till he was dead. But he shouldn't
—he shouldn't—he had means by which
he could escape it yet. Why didn't Hannah
come up to tell him what was going on?
Could she be in league with his tormentors,
after all the protestations she had made to
him an hour ago? Perhaps—it was not
unlikely—women were such arch deceivers,
they would smile in your face one moment,
and draw a knife across your throat the
next. Well! he would escape her too !—
no one should triumph over his public fall.
As he thought thus, Henry Hindes crept
round to his chest of drawers and groped
in the dark for the lock, which he opened

with the keys he kept beneath his pillow.
He found a bottle there—a bottle the
shape of which he knew full well, for had
it not been his daily and nightly companion
for many months past? He knew it, and it
knew him, he said to himself, with a sar-
donic smile, that was half a sneer, and they
had never known each other better, nor
valued each other more, than they would
do that night. But as he was about to
re-enter his bed, he remembered his little
Wally lying in the next room, and thought
he would like to take a look at him first.
So he crept into the adjoining chamber,
where the boy lay fast asleep, with one
arm, thinned by sickness, thrown above his
head. Hindes put his lips reverently on
the little arm and then softly lay down
beside his child.

Meanwhile, Hannah was feeling almost
too thankful for words. How happy she
would make poor Henry when he next
woke. No need for packing up in a hurry
now, and slinking out of England like a
condemned criminal. He might stay on in

safety till he had wound up his own affairs,
and could start for the new land sur-
rounded by his family.

'What a relief! what a relief!' she
thought, as she went upstairs. 'I shall
love and pray for the name of Walcheren
to the last day of my life!'

She peeped into Wally's chamber first!
There lay her child flushed with sleep, and
beside him, with one arm thrown round the
boy's body, was her husband, white and
weary looking, but apparently sound asleep
as well.

'Poor fellow!' mused Hannah, as she
stood and gazed at him. 'He is utterly
worn-out. I wonder what made him fancy
getting into bed with the child. Perhaps
it was to make sure that I should not come
up without waking him. Henry dear,'
she said aloud, as she touched the sleeper
gently. 'Henry! I have such good news,
such lovely news for you. Our worst
troubles are over, darling! Wake up and
hear what I have to tell you!'

She stooped and kissed his cold cheek

as she spoke, and the truth was instantly revealed to her. Her husband slept so deeply that he would never wake in this world again.

At the very moment when his doubts and fears were to be set at rest, he had taken the law into his own hands and gone from this sphere to work out his life's punishment in another.

CHAPTER X.

A FEW days after this occurrence, Rhoda Berry was seated in her mother's cottage at Luton, plaiting straw. It was interesting to watch her deft fingers weaving and interweaving the fine splits of straw, until they formed a plait as delicate as that of a woman's hair. The operation appeared as intricate as that of lace-making, until the ends were worked in and the Grecian pattern became visible.

At her feet sat, or rather tumbled, her baby boy, amusing himself also with the ends of straw his mother dropped. Mrs Berry was bustling in and out of the little kitchen meanwhile, occupied with her domestic duties, and discussing, with some vehemence, the contents of a letter she had received that morning.

' I can't think why you object to the idea,
Rhoda,' she said. ' Here's a fine oppor-
tunity for us both to live like ladies again,
and you almost turn up your nose at it !
My brother Will is not one to go from his
word, and you heard what he said, that
since his wife is dead and he is so lonely,
with his only son at sea, he would be grateful if you and I would take up our abode
at King's Farm for the rest of our lives.
I know what that means, Rhoda ! That
he intends to leave all he has to us. Will
is not the fellow to invite two women to his
house like that, and then leave them to
starve. And this is next door to starvation.
It's drudging from morning to night, and
making a penny how and when we can.
And my brother keeps two house-servants,
fancy that ! And I should have the management of them both ! '

' Mother, dear ! why don't you go, and
leave me here ? I am quite capable of
earning my own living, and you know the
obstacle to my going to King's Farm.
How could I take my baby there, to dis-

grace my uncle and all his family? But it is a shame that my fault should be the means of keeping you from a good home. Do write and accept this offer, mother, and I shall do well enough in Luton, never fear. Why! I'm earning thirty shillings a week now, even in the worst times. I shall do well enough. That's more than sufficient for me and baby. But I'll never take him into another man's house to be scorned and pointed at.'

' Now, Rhoda, what nonsense you talk!' exclaimed Mrs Berry, impatiently. ' As if anything would tempt me to part from you and the little crow! As if you hadn't suffered enough without your mother forsaking you, poor girl! No, I'm not made of such stuff as that! Either we go to King's Farm together, or we don't go at all. But I must say I would like to see the roses back in your cheeks, Rhoda! You used to have such a fine colour before you went up to London. It would do you and the little crow such a world of good, too, to be running about the green fields and lanes of

Somersetshire, and to live amongst the
cows and sheep and chickens. You'd be
another woman in a fortnight.'

' I know I should, mother, but, you see,
this is one of the good things of this life
that I have put away from me by my sin.
It is part of the penance God has called
upon me to perform. And that I must
prevent your taking advantage of Uncle
Will's offer, also, makes it doubly hard to
bear.'

'Why, you don't suppose I could have
any pleasure in it all whilst my only girl
was moping down here by herself, do you?
It's that bothering little crow that sticks in
the way. Suppose we get rid of him,
Rhoda?' said Mrs Berry, playfully. 'Let's
drown him in the water-butt. No one will
be any the wiser, and it would be a blessing to get rid of him, wouldn't it, now?'

She expected to see Rhoda shake her
head sadly at the proposal, but she was
not prepared to see her catch her child up
and press it passionately to her bosom,
whilst she burst into a flood of tears. That

was so unlike her patient, humble, quiet Rhoda, that Mrs Berry was fairly taken aback.

'Why, my dear, my dear,' she cried, 'what is the matter? What have I said to upset you so? I was only in fun, Rhoda. Surely you know that? I wouldn't harm a hair of the child's head for all the wealth of the Indies.'

'Yes, mother, yes; I know it,' replied the girl, still sobbing. 'Only, I feel, I foresee that my poor bairn will be my curse and yours, perhaps, through life. The trouble and the expense are nothing —nothing. But it's the shame that is so hard to bear, not only for myself, but for you and him, poor lamb, when he is old enough to understand.'

'Ay, Rhoda, it's what was pro- phesied long ago—the sins of the fathers being visited on the children, but you mustn't make too much of it. You've had your share of fretting, goodness knows! and you'll kill yourself if you get no rest from it. You're not over strong, my girl, as it is. I've watched your cheeks grow thinner for many a day past, and it's worried me more than enough. This Mr Walcheren is as much dead to you, Rhoda, as if he was in his grave, where I'm sure I wish to goodness he had been before he had ever met you, and so you must try not to think of him, and that's why I'd like to see a few more miles put between you. It does you no good to live so near London.'

'Mother,' said the girl, as she dried her wet eyes, 'if you imagine for a moment that I think of Fred in any other light than that of another woman's husband, you are very much mistaken. If he were free to marry to-morrow, he wouldn't ask *me* to be his wife.'

('More shame for him,' interpolated Mrs Berry.)

'He is grieving too much to dream of marrying again, even if he were in the world. His heart is buried in his wife's grave.'

'More shame for him,' repeated her mother, 'and with that poor little child running about without a father to his name.'

'Such a thing has never entered my imagination for a minute,' continued Rhoda. 'I am glad that we are friends, and proud that he should consider me worthy to give him advice, but there will never be anything more between us. How could there be?'

'I understood he had some idea of leaving the Church.'

'He alluded to it, mother, but I do not suppose he will have the courage to carry it out. It would take the spirit of a hero, or a martyr, to brave the sneers and contempt and abuse of the world for taking such a step. And Frederick was never very strong-minded. He must have altered greatly since I knew him if he has the courage of his own opinions.'

'He's not like you, then, my dear, who have, I verily believe, the courage of a lion. But I mustn't stop chattering any longer, or we shall have no dinner to-day. But think over Uncle Will's proposal

again, Rhoda, before you finally make up
your mind. He's too good a man to
throw a girl's misfortune in her teeth.
And we shall never get such a chance
again—never.'

Rhoda smiled faintly, but she shook her
head all the same. Never had her sin
stared her so unpleasantly in the face
before. To be disgraced for Frederick's
sake—to bear her shame silently and alone
—to have to toil through life to maintain
her child—all this she had realised long
ago, and made up her mind to bear cour-
ageously.

But to stand in the way of her mother's
well-doing—to have to see her toiling, even
to old age, because of her daughter's fault
—to know that she stood between her and
comfort, between her and the love of her
own family, between her and rest, and a
home more fitted to her position than the
one they had occupied since Rhoda's father
died—*this* was the bitterest portion of the
cup she had been called upon to drink.

When Mrs Berry had left her, the poor

girl wept long and bitterly, as she tried to decide whether it might not be her duty to bear the shame and contempt which would be her share if she took her child amongst her mother's relations. It was hard to contemplate. She had hoped the worst was over—that, the inhabitants of Luton having agreed to overlook her misfortune, there would be no more unpleasantness to encounter, but if it was to be for her mother's sake—her dear mother, who had clung to her through everything—she would pass through the fire a second time. It was less than she deserved, she knew that, and, if needful, she would be brave and bear it.

She dried her eyes again, and turned to recommence her work. But the baby had got hold of her plait of straw, which had fallen to the ground, and taken advantage of his mother's abstraction to undo half of it, and spoil the rest.

'Oh, baby, baby!' she cried. 'How naughty you are. You have spoiled poor mother's work.'

As she spoke, and lifted the child in her arms, a shadow darkened the threshold of the open door, and, glancing up, she encountered the eyes of Frederick Walcheren fixed upon her. Rhoda rose in the utmost confusion. She did not know what to say to him. She was as timid of being caught with the child in her arms as if Frederick had never heard of its existence. The first words she stammered were,—

' *You !* Oh, why have you came down here ? '

'Expressly to see you, Rhoda,' he replied, ' seeing that I know no one else in Luton. And so this is the little chap, is it? He is a sturdy fellow. And his eyes and hair are very dark, Rhoda.'

' Yes,' she answered in a low voice.

She could not understand why, under their present circumstances, Frederick should care to allude to the likeness between her child and himself. It jarred upon her. She put the baby down on the ground and began plaiting the straw again.

' Mayn't I come in ? Are you not going

to ask me to sit down ?   I am rather tired,'
said Frederick Walcheren, 'and I have a
good many things to talk to you about.'

'Oh! yes, forgive me,' she replied, as
she rose and set a chair for her visitor at
the opposite side of the little room.

'Are you very much surprised to see
me here, Rhoda ? ' he commenced.

'Yes! very! It is so unexpected. I
don't know what mother will say,' replied
the girl, in an uncertain tone.

'I hope I may be able to relieve her
mind.   But you haven't looked at me,
Rhoda.'

She raised her eyes then, and gave a
little exclamation of surprise.

'Oh! what is changed in you ?   What
have you done to yourself?   You look so
different!'

'Cannot you see?   I am in plain
clothes.'

She recognised the alteration then.   He
wore a rough suit of grey tweed, such as
gentlemen sport in the country, with a
coloured tie, and a round hat.

'You have discarded your cassock! What does this mean? Have you—can you really have left the Church?'

'I have indeed, Rhoda! Whatever my friends or enemies may think of my determination, I have resolved to follow the dictates of my own conscience, and be accountable to no one for my actions except God.'

The soft rose colour mounted to the girl's cheeks with pleasure.

'I am so glad,' she whispered.

'So you ought to be, for it is all your doing. Ever since I saw you last, I have been unable to get those words out of my ears :

> "To thine own self be true,
> It follows, as the night, the day,
> Thou canst not then be false to any man."

I was untrue to myself, Rhoda, when I allowed my friends to persuade me to become a priest, but, at the time, I was in no fit state to judge of anything. But I think I might have remained in it for ever, had it not been for your encouragement and brave advice. I suppose I shall make a great scandal amongst my brethren by leaving it, but they will not make it more public than necessary. The churches always hush up anything that does not redound to their credit. But I am willing, in this case, to take all the blame on myself.'

'And what are you going to do, Fred? You will not prosecute that unfortunate man, I hope,' said Rhoda, wistfully.

'Ah! Rhoda, there is no need to do it! The temptation has been removed from my way. He is dead.'

'*Dead!*' she echoed, wonderingly.

'Yes. It is true. After I left you that evening, I found your persuasions and arguments had taken such hold upon my mind that I resolved to go on to this man's dwelling at once and tell him he had nothing to fear from me.'

'Oh, Fred, how good of you!' cried the girl, with tears in her eyes.

'I did so, therefore, and saw the man's wife, whom I found knew the whole story, and thought I had come to accuse her husband openly of the murder. I set her mind at rest on the subject, and she told me he had determined to leave England the following day. He had retired to rest, so I did not attempt to disturb him, knowing his wife would tell him everything. The next day I received a letter from her to say that, on going up to her husband's room to communicate the news to him, she found him lying dead on the same bed as his little child. She tried to make out his was an ordinary sudden death, but, at the coroner's inquest that followed, I see they brought it in as suicide. Undoubtedly, the poor wretch had taken poison under the fear of detection. I had heard he was greatly addicted to the use of morphia. Remorse had driven him out of his mind.'

'And the poor wife and children—what will become of them?' asked Rhoda.

'They have plenty of this world's goods, child, with which to make themselves comfortable, and the peace of mind, let us hope, will come with time. She has a very kind brother and sister-in-law, who flew to her directly they heard the news of her husband's death, and they will doubtless be her firm friends in the future. And she has three children, Rhoda, to look to for comfort. I am very glad of it, for she is a good woman and wife and mother, and, I am told, believed in him to the last.'

'Poor lady,' sighed Rhoda, 'how sad for her to find him worthless of her regard. The worst thing we can be called upon to bear is, to find our love has been thrown away.'

'As you threw yours away on me, Rhoda.'

'No, I didn't mean that,' she answered, colouring. 'I shouldn't have said it before you if I had.'

'But *I* mean it, Rhoda. I have been a scoundrel to you. I never saw it more plainly than I do to-day, to find you hard at work, with this child crawling at your feet.'

'Don't speak of it, Fred, please. It is past. Let the subject be tabooed between us. What are your plans? Tell me what you intend to do?'

'I am going to leave the country, Rhoda. I don't wish to bring more discredit on my faith and family than I need, so I shall make my home in a new land, and never offend their sight or hearing again. I am penniless, as you know. Every farthing of my fine fortune has gone into the coffers of the Church. I can't say I don't regret it, for I do; but I must accept the loss as part of the penalty of not knowing my own mind.'

'Money does not make all the happiness of this world,' said Rhoda, softly.

'No, but a considerable portion of it. However, least said, in this case, soonest mended. Failing it, I must work with my hands for my daily bread, which, perhaps, will be all the better for me. I shall begin low, but shall hope to rise by-and-by. An old chum of mine has lent me sufficient money to take me out of the country and settle me down a bit, and I am going straight to another chum, who has a big ranche out in the Rocky Mountains, and who, I know, will find me some sort of work to do.'

'But, Fred—' began Rhoda, eagerly.

'Wait a minute, my dear.   I have something more to say to you.   I shall have to go, of course, any way, but you would make me so much happier if you would go with me.'

'*Go with you!*' exclaimed Rhoda, looking up with startled eyes.

'Yes, as my wife, of course.   You didn't suppose I was brute enough to add an insult to the wrong I have done you.'

'But, Fred, I am not worthy,' cried the girl, with crimsoned cheeks.

'Not worthy! Don't make me feel a greater villain than I do, by saying such a thing.   Rhoda, dear, I never deceived you. You know I never made what is called "love" to you in the old, thoughtless days, which ended so disastrously for you.   I didn't love anybody at that time, unless it was myself and my own selfish pleasures. I adored my poor wife.   I am not afraid to say that before you, because you are not like other women. You like a man to speak the truth, not a lot of lies and flattery. But, if ever I loved a woman in my life, you have made me love you. If ever I felt that anyone was absolutely necessary to my existence, I feel that of you. If ever a fellow-creature has been a true, unselfish, trustworthy friend to me, it is you; and I am only speaking the plain truth when I say, if you will come with me to America and share my rough life there, you will make me far happier than I ever expected to be again.'

Rhoda had slipped from her seat and was kneeling by his side, hiding her face upon his hands.

'Oh, my love, my love!' she sobbed, 'I cannot believe it. It is too wonderful for me to believe. Oh! take me with you as your servant, your slave, anything, so as I may remain near you in sickness or health, to look after your comfort and minister to your wants.'

But he raised her up and sat her on his knee.

'As my slave. Yes!' he answered as he kissed her, 'all wives who love their husbands become slaves, but a slave that will be very near my heart, Rhoda—a slave that shall be honoured above everyone in my household. Is that a bargain, my dear? That we shall promise to be true friends and counsellors to our lives' end.'

'Oh! Fred, I am so happy. I never thought or dreamt that it could come to this. I should have been content to be your friend only for ever.'

'Oh, no! you wouldn't,' he said, shaking his head; 'and if you would, I shouldn't. But remember, I am a beggar, Rhoda. All those magic bank-notes, that procured us so much pleasure in the old days, are gone for ever. It is a hard lot I ask you to share with me. You are marrying a gentleman who has nothing but the title to recommend him.'

'But, Fred, it is not so,' said the girl; 'you forget that you made Mr Sinclair invest five thousand pounds for baby. I never touched it, darling! I never should have touched it during your lifetime. I told Mr Sinclair so, and it is there for you to take when you choose. And, though it is little to what you used to have, still, it is better than nothing, isn't it?'

'Better than nothing! I should rather think so! Why, under the circumstances, it is a fortune. But it is not mine, Rhoda! It belongs to the little chap there!'

'Oh, Fred, what nonsense! Who gave it him? Who has a better right to it than you? Besides, you have given him value in exchange, twice told.'

'What is that?' inquired Frederick.

'A father,' she whispered.

At this juncture in bustled Mrs Berry from the kitchen, bearing a smoking beef-steak pudding in her hands.

'Now, Rhoda, my girl, it's past two. Where's the cloth?' she began, but finished up with, 'My gracious! whom have we got here?'

Rhoda was too excited and happy to wait for introductions.

'Mother! mother!' she cried, springing

to Mrs Berry's arms, and nearly upsetting the pudding altogether, 'it's my Fred, and he's going to marry me, and we're going to the Rocky Mountains together, and oh, mother! you will be able to go and keep Uncle Will's house for him now whilst we're away.'

She clung to her mother, sobbing and laughing at the same time, whilst Mrs Berry and Frederick Walcheren could only stand and gaze at one another in astonishment.

'Rhoda, Rhoda, my dear! be reasonable!' at last said Frederick, as he took her hand and tried to pull her away.

'Reasonable! well, I wish she would!' exclaimed Mrs Berry; 'how am I to be expected to understand all this scrimmage, when you've never had the decency to tell me the man was in the house? *Your* Fred, indeed! Why, I thought your Fred was a Roman priest. Are you imposing on me, child? and putting another young man on me instead of him?'

'No, no! indeed, mother!' said Rhoda,

as she caught up her baby, and prepared to leave the room. 'Oh, Fred! explain the whole thing to mother, and I'll be back in a minute.'

She flew upstairs, and spent some time crying and cooing over her child, and telling him, amidst her frantic kisses, what a dear, good father he had, and how very, very much his mother loved them both. She bathed her own eyes, too, and smoothed her golden hair, and descended to the little parlour, blushing like a rose, but with eyes beaming with gratitude and affection.

'Well, here's a pretty kettle of fish!' exclaimed Mrs Berry, as her daughter appeared; 'and so you're to be off to the United States in another fortnight, and leave your poor mother to go to King's Farm by herself. A nice, dutiful daughter you are, upon my word!'

'Oh, mother darling! you know it is the very thing you would have chosen had you been given your wish!' said the girl. It is sad to part, dear, but it is all for the best! You will be so happy and comfortable with Uncle Will, and the next time I see England,' she added, in a whisper, 'I shall not be ashamed, you know, to go down and pay you and him a visit.'

'Ah, my poor lamb!' said her mother, looking fondly at her. 'Thank God! the shame you have borne so bravely is to be lifted off your brow at last. Mr Walcheren, she has been a true and steadfast wife to you! God grant you may reward her!'

Frederick Walcheren stretched out his hand, and drew Rhoda and her child within the shelter of his arms.

'May God forsake me,' he answered, 'if I ever make her weep again!'

THE END.

COLSTON AND COMPANY, PRINTERS, EDINBURGH.

LIST OF PUBLICATIONS.

14 *Bedford Street,*

Strand,

London, W.C.

F. V. WHITE & CO.'S

LIST OF

PUBLICATIONS

NEW
NOVELS AT ALL CIRCULATING LIBRARIES.

THE SOUL OF THE BISHOP. By JOHN STRANGE WINTER, Author of "Bootles' Baby," "The Other Man's Wife," "Army Society," &c. 2 vols.

A TRAGIC BLUNDER. By Mrs LOVETT CAMERON, Author of "In a Grass Country," Jack's Secret," "A Daughter's Heart," &c. 2 vols.

THE HAMPSTEAD MYSTERY. By FLORENCE MARRYAT, Author of "My Sister the Actress," "Facing the Foot-lights," "The Heart of Jane Warner," &c. 3 vols.

THE HUNTING GIRL. By Mrs EDWARD KENNARD, Author of "The Girl in the Brown Habit," Wedded to Sport," "A Homburg Beauty," &c. 3 vols.

A THIRD PERSON. By B. M. CROKER, Author of "Proper Pride " "Interference," "Two Masters," &c. 2 vols.

FOUND WANTING. By Mrs ALEXANDER, Author of "The Wooing o't," "For His Sake," "A Woman's Heart," &c. 3 vols.

FOR ONE SEASON ONLY. A Sporting Novel. By Mrs ROBERT JOCELYN, Author of "The M.F.H.'s Daughter," "Drawn Blank," &c. 3 vols.

THE SORCERESS. By Mrs OLIPHANT. Author of "The Heir Presumptive and the Heir Apparent," "The Cuckoo in the Nest," "The Son of his Father," &c. 3 vols.

UTTERLY MISTAKEN. BY ANNIE THOMAS (Mrs Pender Cudlip), Author of "Allerton Towers," "Denis Donne," "Eyre of Blendon," &c. 3 vols.

THE COUNTESS PHARAMOND: A Sequel to "Sheba" By "Rita," Author of "Dame Durden," "The Laird o' Cockpen," &c. 3 vols.

A GIRL'S PAST. By Mrs HERBERT MARTIN, Author of "Bonnie Lesley," "A Man and a Brother," "Common Clay," &c. 3 vols.

AUNT JOHNNIE. By JOHN STRANGE WINTER, 2 vols.

F. V. WHITE & Co., 14 Bedford Street, Strand.

THE WORKS OF JOHN STRANGE WINTER.

UNIFORM IN STYLE AND PRICE.

(At all Booksellers' and Bookstalls.)   In Paper Covers, 1s.; Cloth, 1s. 6d.

WINTER'S CHRISTMAS ANNUAL.
(9th year of Publication), entitled "A MAN'S MAN."

THAT MRS SMITH.   (2d Edition.)

THREE GIRLS.   (3d Edition.)

MERE LUCK.   (3d Edition.)

LUMLEY THE PAINTER.   (3d Edition.)

GOOD-BYE.   (7th Edition.)

HE WENT FOR A SOLDIER.   (8th Edition.)

FERRERS COURT.   (6th Edition.)

BUTTONS.   (7th Edition).

A LITTLE FOOL.   (10th Edition.)

MY POOR DICK.   (Illustrated by MAURICE GRIEF-FENHAGEN.)   (9th Edition.)

BOOTLES' CHILDREN.   (Illustrated by J. BERNARD PARTRIDGE.)   (11th Edition.)

"John Strange Winter is never more thoroughly at home than when delineating the characters of children, and everyone will be delighted with the dignified Madge and the quaint Pearl. The book is mainly occupied with the love affairs of Terry (the soldier servant who appears in many of the preceding books), but the children buzz in and out of its pages much as they would come in and out of a room in real life, pervading and brightening the house in which they dwell."—*Leicester Daily Post.*

THE CONFESSIONS OF A PUBLISHER.

"The much discussed question of the relations between a publisher and his clients furnishes Mr John Strange Winter with material for one of the brightest tales of the season. Abel Drinkwater's autobiography is written from a humorous point of view ; yet here, as elsewhere, 'many a true word is spoken in jest,' and in the conversations of the publisher and his too ingenuous son, facts come to light that are worthy of the attention of aspirants to literary fame."—*Morning Post.*

MIGNON'S HUSBAND.   (14th Edition.)

"It is a capital love story, full of high spirits, and written in a dashing style that will charm the most melancholy of readers into hearty enjoyment of its fun."—*Scotsman.*

THAT IMP.   (12th Edition.)

"Barrack life is abandoned for the nonce, and the author of 'Bootles' Baby' introduces readers to a country home replete with every comfort and containing men and women whose acquaintanceship we can only regret can never blossom into friendship."—*Whitehall Review.*

"This charming little book is bright and breezy, and has the ring of supreme truth about it."—*Vanity Fair.*

MIGNON'S SECRET.   (17th Edition.)

"In 'Mignon's Secret' Mr Winter has supplied a continuation to the never-to-be-forgotten 'Bootles' Baby.' . . . The story is gracefully and touchingly told."—*John Bull.*

F. V. WHITE & Co., 14 Bedford Street, Strand.

The Works of JOHN STRANGE WINTER—*Continued.*

ON MARCH. (10th Edition.)

" This short story is characterised by Mr Winter's customary truth in detail, humour, and pathos."—*Academy.*

" By publishing 'On March,' Mr J. S. Winter has added another little gem to his well-known store of regimental sketches. The story is written with humour and a deal of feeling."—*Army and Navy Gazette.*

IN QUARTERS. (11th Edition.)

" ' In Quarters' is one of those rattling tales of soldiers' life which the public have learned to thoroughly appreciate."—*The Graphic.*

"The author of ' Bootles' Baby ' gives us here another story of military life, which few have better described."—*British Quarterly Review.*

ARMY SOCIETY: Life in a Garrison Town.

Cloth, 6s. ; in Picture Boards, 2s. (10th Edition.)

" This discursive story, dealing with life in a garrison town, is full of pleasant ' go' and movement which has distinguished ' Bootles' Baby,' ' Pluck,' or, in fact, a majority of some half-dozen novelettes which the author has submitted to the eyes of railway bookstall patronisers."—*Daily Telegraph.*

" The strength of the book lies in its sketches of life in a garrison town, which are undeniably clever. . . . It is pretty clear that Mr Winter draws from life."—*St James's Gazette.*

GARRISON GOSSIP, Gathered in Blankhampton.

(A Sequel to "ARMY SOCIETY.") Cloth, 2s. 6d. ; in Picture Boards, 2s. (6th Edition.)

" ' Garrison Gossip' may fairly rank with ' Cavalry Life,' and the various other books with which Mr Winter has so agreeably beguiled our leisure hours."—*Saturday Review.*

" The novel fully maintains the reputation which its author has been fortunate enough to gain in a special line of his own."—*Graphic.*

A SIEGE BABY.

Cloth, 2s. 6d. ; Picture Boards, 2s. (5th Edition.)

' The story which gives its title to this new sheaf of stories by the popular author of ' Bootles' Baby ' is a very touching and pathetic one. . . . Amongst the other stories, the one entitled ' Out of the Mists' is, perhaps, the best written, although the tale of true love it embodies comes to a most melancholy ending."—*County Gentleman.*

BEAUTIFUL JIM. (8th Edition.)

Cloth, 2s. 6d. ; Picture Boards, 2s.

MRS BOB. (7th Edition.)

Cloth, 2s. 6d. ; Picture Boards, 2s.

THE OTHER MAN'S WIFE. (5th Edition.)

Cloth, 2s. 6d. Picture Boards, 2s.

MY GEOFF ; or, The Experiences of a Lady Help.

A New Novel. (5th Edition.) Cloth, 2s. 6d.; Picture Boards, 2s.

ONLY HUMAN. (3d Edition.) Cloth, 2s. 6d.

MRS EDWARD KENNARD'S SPORTING NOVELS.

(At all Booksellers' and Bookstalls.)

WEDDED TO SPORT. Cloth gilt, 3s. 6d.
SPORTING TALES. (A new Novel). Cl. gilt, 2s. 6d.
TWILIGHT TALES. (Illustrated.) Cl. gilt, 2s. 6d.

Cloth gilt, 2s. 6d.   Picture Boards, 2s.

THAT PRETTY LITTLE HORSE-BREAKER.
(4th Edition.)

A HOMBURG BEAUTY. (3d Edition.)

MATRON OR MAID? (4th Edition.)

LANDING A PRIZE. (7th Edition.)

A CRACK COUNTY. (6th Edition.)

THE GIRL IN THE BROWN HABIT.
(8th Edition.)

"'Nell Fitzgerald'" is an irreproachable heroine, full of gentle womanliness, and rich in all virtues that make her kind estimable. Mrs Kennard's work is marked by high tone as well as vigorous narrative, and sportsmen, when searching for something new and beguiling for a wet day or spell of frost, can hardly light upon anything better than these fresh and picturesque hunting stories of Mrs Kennard's."—*Daily Telegraph.*

KILLED IN THE OPEN. (9th Edition.)

" It is in truth a very good love story set in a framework of hounds and horses, but one that could be read with pleasure independently of any such attractions. '—*Fortnightly Review.*

" ' Killed in the Open ' is a very superior sort of hunting novel indeed."—*Graphic.*

STRAIGHT AS A DIE. (8th Edition.)

" If you like sporting novels I can recommend to you Mrs Kennard's ' Straight as a Die.'"—*Truth.*

A REAL GOOD THING. (8th Edition.)

"There are some good country scenes and country spins in 'A Real Good Thing.' The hero, poor old Hopkins, is a strong character."—*Academy.*

OUR FRIENDS IN THE HUNTING-FIELD.

BY THE SAME AUTHOR.

THE MYSTERY OF A WOMAN'S HEART.   In
Paper Covers, 1s. ; Cloth, 1s. 6d.

F. V. WHITE & Co., 14 Bedford Street, Strand.

HAWLEY SMART'S SPORTING NOVELS.
(At all Booksellers' and Bookstalls.)

Cloth gilt, 2s. 6d.   Picture Boards, 2s.

BEATRICE AND BENEDICK: A Romance of the
Crimea. (2d Edition.)
THE PLUNGER. (5th Edition)
LONG ODDS. (5th Edition.)
THE MASTER OF RATHKELLY. (5th Edition.)
THE OUTSIDER. (8th Edition.)
VANITY'S DAUGHTER.   Paper, 1s. ; Cloth, 1s. 6d.

NOVELS BY B. L. FARJEON.
(At all Booksellers' and Bookstalls.)
Cloth, 2s. 6d.   Picture Boards, 2s. each.

THE MARCH OF FATE. (Cloth only.)
BASIL AND ANNETTE. (2d Edition.)
THE MYSTERY OF M. FELIX.
A YOUNG GIRL'S LIFE. (3d Edition.)
TOILERS OF BABYLON. (2d Edition.)
THE DUCHESS OF ROSEMARY LANE. (2d Edit.)

In Paper Covers, 1s.   Cloth 1s. 6d. each.

A VERY YOUNG COUPLE.
THE PERIL OF RICHARD PARDON. (2d Edition.)
A STRANGE ENCHANTMENT.

By B. M. CROKER.
(At all Booksellers' and Bookstalls.)

INTERFERENCE. (2d Edition.)   Cloth, 2s. 6d.
TWO MASTERS. (3d Edition.)   2s. 6d. and 2s.

By HELEN MATHERS.
(At all Booksellers' and Bookstalls.)
In Paper Covers, 1s.   Cloth, 1s. 6d. each.

WHAT THE GLASS TOLD.
A STUDY OF A WOMAN.
T'OTHER DEAR CHARMER.
MY JO, JOHN. (2d Edition.)
THE MYSTERY OF No. 13. (2d Edition.)

Sir RANDAL H. ROBERTS, Bart.'s, Sporting Novels

(At all Booksellers' and Bookstalls.)

NOT IN THE BETTING. (A New Novel.)   Cloth gilt, 2s. 6d.
CURB AND SNAFFLE.   Cloth gilt, 2s. 6d.

By Mrs ALEXANDER FRASER.

(At all Booksellers' and Bookstalls.)

A MODERN BRIDEGROOM. (2d Edition.)   Cloth, 2s. 6d.
THE NEW DUCHESS. (2d Edition.)   Cloth, 2s. 6d.
DAUGHTERS OF BELGRAVIA.   Cloth, 2s. 6d.   Picture Boards, 2s.
SHE CAME BETWEEN.   Cloth, 2s. 6d.

MRS LOVETT CAMERON'S NOVELS.

(At all Booksellers' and Bookstalls.)

A SISTER'S SIN.   Cloth, 2s. 6d.
IN A GRASS COUNTRY. (A Story of Love of Sport.) (10th
    Edition.)   Cl. gilt, 2s. 6d.; Picture Boards, 2s.; Paper Covers, 1s.

" We turn with pleasure to the green covers of ' In a Grass Country.' The three heroines are charming, each in her own way. It is well sketched, full of character, with sharp observations of men and women—not too hard on anybody—a clear story, carefully written, and therefore easily read. . . . recommended."—*Punch.*

"When the days are short and there is an hour or two to be disposed of indoors before dressing time, one is glad to be able to recommend a good and amusing novel. 'In a Grass Country' may be said to come under this description."— *Saturday Review.*

WEAK WOMAN. (2d Edition.)   Cloth, 2s. 6d.
JACK'S SECRET. (3d Edition.)   Cloth, 2s. 6d.; Picture Boards, 2s.
A LOST WIFE. (3d Edition.)   Cloth, 2s. 6d.; Picture Boards, 2s.
A DAUGHTER'S HEART.   Cloth, 2s. 6d

By JUSTIN M'CARTHY, M.P., and Mrs CAMPBELL PRAED.

(Authors of "The Right Honourable," &c.)

(At all Booksellers' and Bookstalls.)

THE RIVAL PRINCESS; a London Romance of
To-day. (3d Edition.)   Cloth, 2s. 6d. ; Picture Boards, 2s.

By MRS CAMPBELL PRAED.

(At all Booksellers' and Bookstalls.)

THE ROMANCE OF A CHÂLET.   Cloth, 2s. 6d.

By Mrs J. H. RIDDELL.

A SILENT TRAGEDY.   Paper Covers, 1s.; Cloth, 1s. 6d.

MRS ALEXANDER'S NOVELS.

(At all Booksellers' and Bookstalls.)

FOR HIS SAKE. Cloth, 2s. 6d.

A WOMAN'S HEART. Cloth, 2s. 6d.

BLIND FATE. Cloth, 2s. 6d.; Picture Boards, 2s.

BY WOMAN'S WIT. (6th Edition.) Cloth, 2s. 6d.; Picture Boards, 2s.

> "In Mrs Alexander's tale
> Much art she clearly shows
> In keeping dark the mystery
> Until the story's close."—*Punch.*

NOVELS BY HUME NISBET.

(At all Booksellers' and Bookstalls.)

THE HAUNTED STATION and other Stories. Cloth gilt, 2s. 6d.

THE QUEEN'S DESIRE ; A Romance of the Indian Mutiny. With Illustrations by the Author. Cloth, 3s. 6d.

THE BUSHRANGER'S SWEETHEART ; An Australian Romance. Cloth, 2s. 6d.; Picture Boards, 2s. (5th Edition.)

THE SAVAGE QUEEN ; A Romance of the Natives of Van Dieman's Land. Cloth, 2s. 6d.; Picture Boards, 2s. (3d Edition.)

"RITA'S" NOVELS.

(At all Booksellers' and Bookstalls.)

THE MAN IN POSSESSION. (A new Novel.) Cloth, 2s. 6d.

THE LAIRD O' COCKPEN. Cloth, 2s. 6d.

MISS KATE. (4th Edit.) Cloth, 2s. 6d.; Picture Boards, 2s.

THE SEVENTH DREAM. 1s. and 1s. 6d.

THE DOCTOR'S SECRET. (2d Edition.) 1s. and 1s. 6d.

By AMYE READE, Author of "Ruby," &c.

(At all Booksellers' and Bookstalls.)

SLAVES OF THE SAWDUST. A New and Original Story of Acrobat Life. By the Author of "Ruby," &c. Picture Boards, 2s.; also Cloth, 2s. 6d. (Dedicated to the late Lord Tennyson.)

F. V. WHITE & Co., 14 Bedford Street, Strand.

POPULAR WORKS.

By MRS HUMPHRY

(" *Madge* " *of* " *Truth* ").

HOUSEKEEPING;

A GUIDE TO DOMESTIC MANAGEMENT.

Cloth Gilt, 3s. 6d.

(At all Booksellers' and Bookstalls.)

By WILLIAM DAY.

Author of "The Racehorse in Training," "Reminiscences of the Turf," &c.

TURF CELEBRITIES I HAVE KNOWN.

WITH A PORTRAIT OF THE AUTHOR.

1 *Vol.*, *gilt cloth.* 16s.

(At all Libraries and Booksellers'.)

By GUSTAV FREYTAG.

REMINISCENCES OF MY LIFE.

Translated from the German by KATHARINE CHETWYND.

In Two Vols. 18s.

(At all Libraries and Booksellers'.)

By MRS ARMSTRONG.

Author of "Modern Etiquette in Public and Private," &c.

GOOD FORM.

A BOOK OF EVERY DAY ETIQUETTE.

(Second Edition.) *Limp Cloth, 2s.*

(At all Booksellers' and Bookstalls.)

By PERCY THORPE.

HISTORY OF JAPAN.

Cloth, 3s. 6d.

(At all Booksellers' and Bookstalls.)

F. V. WHITE & Co., 14 Bedford Street, Strand.

ONE VOLUME NOVELS

BY POPULAR AUTHORS.

Crown 8vo, Cloth, 2s. 6d. each.

(AT ALL BOOKSELLERS' AND BOOKSTALLS.)

By JOHN STRANGE WINTER.

ONLY HUMAN. | BEAUTIFUL JIM.
MY GEOFF. | A SIEGE BABY.
THE OTHER MAN'S WIFE. | GARRISON GOSSIP.
MRS BOB. |

By MRS EDWARD KENNARD.

WEDDED TO SPORT, 3s. 6d. | SPORTING TALES.
TWILIGHT TALES. (A New Novel.)
THAT PRETTY LITTLE HORSE-BREAKER.
A HOMBURG BEAUTY. | A CRACK COUNTY.
MATRON OR MAID? | A REAL GOOD THING.
LANDING A PRIZE. | STRAIGHT AS A DIE.
THE GIRL IN THE BROWN HABIT.
KILLED IN THE OPEN.
OUR FRIENDS IN THE HUNTING-FIELD.

By HAWLEY SMART.

BEATRICE AND BENEDICK.
THE PLUNGER. | THE MASTER OF RATHKELLY.
LONG ODDS. | THE OUTSIDER.

By MRS CAMPBELL PRAED.

THE ROMANCE OF A CHALET.

By B. L. FARJEON.

THE MYSTERY OF M. FELIX.
THE MARCH OF FATE. | A YOUNG GIRL'S LIFE.
TOILERS OF BABYLON. | BASIL AND ANNETTE.
THE DUCHESS OF ROSEMARY LANE.

By MAY CROMMELIN.

THE FREAKS OF LADY FORTUNE.

By FLORENCE WARDEN.

A YOUNG WIFE'S TRIAL; or, RALPH RYDER of BRENT.
A WITCH OF THE HILLS. | A WILD WOOING.

By MABEL COLLINS.

VIOLA FANSHAWE.

By B. M. CROKER.

TWO MASTERS. | INTERFERENCE.

By HUME NISBET.

THE HAUNTED STATION and other Stories.
THE QUEEN'S DESIRE (Cloth, 3s. 6d.) | THE SAVAGE QUEEN.
THE BUSHRANGER'S SWEETHEART.

ONE VOLUME NOVELS—*Continued.*

By SIR RANDAL-ROBERTS, Bart.
NOT IN THE BETTING. (A New Novel.)
CURB AND SNAFFLE.

By AMYE READE.
SLAVES OF THE SAWDUST.

By F. C. PHILIPS and C. J. WILLS.
SYBIL ROSS'S MARRIAGE.

By MRS ALEXANDER.
BLIND FATE.	BY WOMAN'S WIT.
A WOMAN'S HEART.	FOR HIS SAKE.

By MRS LOVETT CAMERON.
A SISTER'S SIN.	A LOST WIFE.
IN A GRASS COUNTRY.	A DAUGHTER'S HEART.
JACK'S SECRET.	WEAK WOMAN.

By JUSTIN M'CARTHY, M.P., and MRS CAMPBELL PRAED.
THE RIVAL PRINCESS.

By MRS ROBERT JOCELYN.
THE M.F.H.'S DAUGHTER.
THE CRITON HUNT MYSTERY.	DRAWN BLANK.
ONLY A HORSE-DEALER.	A BIG STAKE.

By BRET HARTE.
THE CRUSADE OF THE "EXCELSIOR."

By the Hon. MRS FETHERSTONHAUGH.
DREAM FACES.

By FERGUS HUME.
WHOM GOD HATH JOINED. | THE MAN WITH A SECRET.

By MRS HUNGERFORD, Author of "Molly Bawn."
THE HON. MRS VEREKER. | APRIL'S LADY.
LADY PATTY. (A New Novel.)

By "RITA."
THE MAN IN POSSESSION.	MISS KATE
(A New Novel.)	THE LAIRD O' COCKPEN.

By MRS ALEXANDER FRASER.
DAUGHTERS OF BELGRAVIA.	THE NEW DUCHESS.
A MODERN BRIDEGROOM.	SHE CAME BETWEEN.

By FLORENCE MARRYAT.
MY SISTER THE ACTRESS.

By MAY CROMMELIN and J. MORAY BROWN.
VIOLET VYVIAN, M.F.H.

By F. C. PHILIPS and PERCY FENDALL.
A DAUGHTER'S SACRIFICE.
MARGARET BYNG. | MY FACE IS MY FORTUNE.

POPULAR NOVELS.

Picture Boards, 2s. each.

At all Booksellers and Bookstalls.

MY GEOFF. (5th Edition.) By John Strange Winter.

THE OTHER MAN'S WIFE. (5th Edition.) By the same Author.

MRS BOB. (7th Edition.) By the same Author.

BEAUTIFUL JIM. (8th Edition.) By the same Author.

A SIEGE BABY. (5th Edition.) By the same Author.

GARRISON GOSSIP. (6th Edition.) By the same Author.

ARMY SOCIETY. Life in a Garrison Town. (10th Edition.) By the same Author.

THE MAN WITH A SECRET. (3d Edition.) By Fergus Hume.

LONG ODDS. (5th Edition.) By Hawley Smart.

THE PLUNGER. (5th Edition.) By the same Author.

THE MASTER OF RATHKELLY. (5th Edition.) By the same Author.

BEATRICE AND BENEDICK. (2d Edition.) By the same Author.

THE OUTSIDER. (8th Edition.) By the same Author.

A LOST WIFE. (3d Edition.) By Mrs Lovett Cameron.

IN A GRASS COUNTRY. (10th Edition.) By the same Author.

JACK'S SECRET. (3d Edition.) By the same Author.

BLIND FATE. By Mrs Alexander.

BY WOMAN'S WIT. (6th Edition.) By the same Author.

THE HON. MRS VEREKER. By Mrs Hungerford, Author of "Molly Bawn."

APRIL'S LADY. (3d Edition.) By the same Author.

LANDING A PRIZE. (7th Edition.) By Mrs Edward Kennard.

THAT PRETTY LITTLE HORSE-BREAKER. (4th Edition.) By the same Author.

A HOMBURG BEAUTY. (3d Edition.) By the same Author.

MATRON OR MAID? (4th Edition.) By the same Author.

A CRACK COUNTY. (6th Edition.) By the same Author.

A REAL GOOD THING. (8th Edition.) By the same Author.

STRAIGHT AS A DIE. (8th Edition.) By the same Author.

THE GIRL IN THE BROWN HABIT. (8th Edition.) By the same Author.

OUR FRIENDS IN THE HUNTING-FIELD. By the same Author.

KILLED IN THE OPEN. (9th Edition.) By the same Author.

POPULAR NOVELS—*Continued.*

TWO MASTERS. (3rd Edition.) By B. M. CROKER.

MISS KATE ; or, Confessions of a Caretaker. (4th Edition.) By " RITA."

TOILERS OF BABYLON. (2d Edition.) By B. L. FARJEON.

THE DUCHESS OF ROSEMARY LANE. (2d Edition.) By the same Author.

THE MYSTERY OF M. FELIX. By the same Author.

A YOUNG GIRL'S LIFE. (3d Edition.) By the same Author.

BASIL AND ANNETTE. (3d Edition.) By the same Author.

THE RIVAL PRINCESS. (3d Edition.) By JUSTIN M'CARTHY, M.P., and Mrs CAMPBELL PRAED.

A WOMAN'S FACE. By FLORENCE WARDEN, Author of " The House on the Marsh," &c.

A WITCH OF THE HILLS. (3d Edition.) By the same Author.

VIOLET VYVIAN, M.F.H. (3d Edition.) By MAY CROMMELIN and J. MORAY BROWN.

THE FREAKS OF LADY FORTUNE. By MAY CROMMELIN.

DAUGHTERS OF BELGRAVIA. By Mrs ALEXANDER FRASER.

SYBIL ROSS'S MARRIAGE : The Romance of an Inexperienced Girl. (3d Edition.) By F. C. PHILIPS and C. J. WILLS.

A DAUGHTER'S SACRIFICE. (3d Edition.) By F. C. PHILIPS and PERCY FENDALL.

MARGARET BYNG. By the same Authors.

THE HEART OF JANE WARNER. By FLORENCE MARRYAT.

MY SISTER THE ACTRESS. By the same Author.

UNDER THE LILIES AND ROSES. By the same Author.

KATE VALLIANT. By ANNIE THOMAS (Mrs PENDER CUDLIP).

MATED WITH A CLOWN. By LADY CONSTANCE HOWARD.

KEITH'S WIFE. By LADY VIOLET GREVILLE.

THE CRUSADE OF THE "EXCELSIOR." By BRET HARTE.

SLAVES OF THE SAWDUST. (A New and Original Work.) By AMYE READE, Author of "Ruby," &c.

NOT EASILY JEALOUS. By IZA DUFFUS HARDY.

ONLY A LOVE STORY. By the same Author.

POISONED ARROWS. By JEAN MIDDLEMASS.

THE SAVAGE QUEEN : A Romance of the Natives of Van Dieman's Land. (3d Edition.) By HUME NISBET.

THE BUSHRANGER'S SWEETHEART. An Australian Romance. (5th Edition.) By the same Author.

THE M.F.H.'S DAUGHTER. By Mrs ROBERT JOCELYN.

THE CRITON HUNT MYSTERY. By the same Author.

F. V. WHITE & Co., 14 Bedford Street, Strand.

ONE SHILLING NOVELS.

In Paper Covers ; Cloth, 1s. 6d.   (At all Booksellers' and Bookstalls.)

WINTER'S CHRISTMAS ANNUAL. (9th year of
Publication), entitled, "A Man's Man." By JOHN
STRANGE WINTER, Author of "Bootles' Baby," &c.

THAT MRS SMITH. (2d Edit.) By the same Author.

THREE GIRLS. (3d Edit.) By the same Author.

MERE LUCK. (3d Edition.) By the same Author.

LUMLEY THE PAINTER. (3d Edition.) By the
same Author.

GOOD-BYE. (7th Edition.) By the same Author.

HE WENT FOR A SOLDIER. (8th Edition.) By
the same Author.

FERRERS COURT. (6th Edit.) By the same Author.

BUTTONS. (7th Edition.) By the same Author.

A LITTLE FOOL. (10th Edit.) By the same Author.

MY POOR DICK. (Illustrated by MAURICE GREIF-
FENHAGEN.) (9th Edition.) By the same Author.

BOOTLES' CHILDREN. (Illustrated by J. BERNARD
PARTRIDGE.) (11th Edition.) By the same Author.

THE CONFESSIONS OF A PUBLISHER. By
the same Author.

MIGNON'S HUSBAND. (14th Edition.) By the
same Author.

THAT IMP. (12th Edition.) By the same Author.

MIGNON'S SECRET. (17th Edition.) By the same
Author.

ON MARCH. (10th Edition.) By the same Author.

IN QUARTERS. (11th Edit.) By the same Author.

THE GENTLEMAN WHO VANISHED. (2d
Edition.) By FERGUS HUME.

THE PICCADILLY PUZZLE. By the same Author.

THE POWER OF AN EYE. By Mrs F. ST CLAIR
GRIMWOOD, Author of "My Three Years in Manipur."

A VERY YOUNG COUPLE. By B. L. FARJEON,
Author of "Toilers of Babylon," &c.

ONE SHILLING NOVELS--*Continued.*

THE PERIL OF RICHARD PARDON. (2d Edition.) By B. L. FARJEON.

A STRANGE ENCHANTMENT. By the same Author.

A SILENT TRAGEDY. By Mrs J. H. RIDDELL, Author of "George Geith of Fen Court," &c.

THE MYSTERY OF NO. 13. (2d Edit.) By ELLEN MATHERS, Author of "Comin' Thro' the Rye," &c.

WHAT THE GLASS TOLD. By the same Author.

A STUDY OF A WOMAN; or, Venus Victrix. By the same Author.

MY JO, JOHN. (2nd Edition.) By the same Author.

T'OTHER DEAR CHARMER. By the same Author.

TOM'S WIFE. By Lady MARGARET MAJENDIE, Author of "Fascination," "Sisters-in-Law," &c.

THE CONFESSIONS OF A DOOR MAT. By AL-FRED C. CALMOUR, Author of "The Amber Heart," &c.

THE MYSTERY OF A WOMAN'S HEART. By Mrs EDWARD KENNARD.

IN A GRASS COUNTRY. By Mrs LOVETT CAMERON. (9th Edition.)

CITY AND SUBURBAN. (2d Edition.) By FLORENCE WARDEN, Author of "The House on the Marsh," &c.

GRAVE LADY JANE. by the same Author.

THE DOCTOR'S SECRET. (2d Edition.) By "RITA," Author of "Dame Durden," "Sheba," &c.

THE SEVENTH DREAM. By the same Author.

VANITY'S DAUGHTER. By HAWLEY SMART.

A CONQUERING HEROINE. By Mrs HUNGERFORD, Author of "Molly Bawn," &c.

A MAD PRANK. By the same Author.

THE MYSTERY OF BELGRAVE SQUARE. By CURTIS YORKE, Author of "Hush!" "A Romance of Modern London," &c. (In cloth only).

A FRENCH MARRIAGE. By F. C. PHILIPS.

FACING THE FOOTLIGHTS. By FLORENCE MARRYAT.